RACING HOME

New

Stories

By

Award-

Winning

 North

 Carolina

Writers

For Ellen,
Don't let the
bastards get you
down!
Warmly,
Anne

Edited by Sharlene Baker
Foreword by Randall Kenan

For my sister, Kathy, with love
and great admiration

acknowledgements

The editor gratefully acknowledges
Lula Griffin, Barbara E. Williams,
Kelley Breeze, Mayapriya Long, Carol Stanley,
Kim Pyne, Karen Stewart, Mike Brown,
Katie Wu, Tommy Gibson, Deborah Wong and
Zoe "The Amazing" Mulford

from the editor

I had this idea clamber into my head in the wee hours of the morning: *Racing Home*! Yes! There can never be enough North Carolina short story collections! I had to make it happen.

Short story writers are some of the most highly gifted — and unnoticed — artists walking among us in the US. What's happened?

Sure, we recognize their names...but only if they also write novels. Though we appear to be reading as many novels as ever, the written short story is losing ground to the short story of the half-hour television show. Fewer and fewer magazines publish short fiction.

As a long-time Triangle area instructor of creative writing, time and again I've come upon short-fiction writers with the ability to unfold tales of such startling clarity and heart I'm struck dizzy. How tragic that many of their manuscripts end up in folders in dark filing cabinets — or worse, 86ed in frustration. There simply are not enough outlets for their work.

My call for works from *award-winning* North Carolina fiction writers brought me a teetering stack of submissions and a pleasant reminder that we *are* "the state of the arts". Those awards were gifts of support from individual patrons, organizations, and from the people of North Carolina, who long have harbored a fierce pride of, and feeling of warm kinship with their writers.

The Paper Journey Press is proud to have the opportunity to publish this volume, not only to present to the public the stories of Award-Winning North Carolina Writers, but also to honor the many art councils, foundations, clubs, associations, publications, universities and all other groups and individuals who have helped to nurture them.

Sharlene Baker, 2001

•Anson County Writer's Club
•Arts Council of Winston-Salem and Forsyth County
•Barton College
•Carnegie Foundation
•Central Piedmont Region of the NC Arts Council
•Charlotte Writer's Club
•Charlotte-Mecklenburg Arts and Science Council
•Chrysler Museum of Art
•Doris Betts
•Durham Arts Council
•The Eugene O'Neill Foundation
•George Mason University's *Phoebe* Literary Magazine
•Greensboro Arts Council
•John Simon Guggenheim Memorial Foundation
•Kentucky Foundation for Women
•Literal Latte Fiction Magazine
•National Academy of Television Arts and Sciences
•National Endowment for the Arts
•*Native Peoples* magazine

•North Carolina Arts Council
•North Carolina Poetry Society
•North Carolina Writers Network
•Pulitzer Board
•Pushcart Prize Committee
•Robert Ruark Foundation
•St. Andrews College Press
•Southern Anthology
•State of North Carolina Department of Administration Council for Women
•Sundance Institute
•Syvenna Foundation, Texas
•Tennessee Williams/ New Orleans Literary Festival
•Triad Arts Council
•Union County Writer's Club
•University of North Carolina, Greensboro, Creative Writing Program
•Virginia Center for the Creative Arts
•Wachovia Bank
•West Virginia Commission on the Arts
•Writers Guild of America
•Wurlitzer Foundation

foreword by
Randall Kenan

I got the letter sometime in the spring. It came to inform me
that my poem, "Who Really Invented the Airplane?" had received an honorable mention in a contest of North Carolina elementary school students and would be included in an anthology.

I never saw that book; I don't know if it ever got published.
But I did get that letter, and it was one of the most memorable
epistles of my life.

This happened in the mid-70s, during the Ford administration. For my poems I used a fluorescent green notebook paper,
with brilliant emerald lines. I kept my carefully copied poems
folded in a plastic pencil holder decorated with psychedelic stick-
ers. I was in the sixth grade, and was fascinated with heavier-than-
air flight. The poem in question was inspired after reading about
all the attempts to create a flying machine before the Wright
Brothers made their historic defiance of gravity at Kitty Hawk,
and how some believed that a few engineering geniuses had
achieved true flight before them. (A view North Carolina historical institutions have a stake in refuting.) The poem was of uncer-
tain meter, and reveled in tortured rhyming couplets, and I revised and revised it. When our English teacher had asked for
sample poems for some mysterious purpose (A writing contest?
What is that? Do you make the stories race?) I gave her this pre-

cocious piece of science-struck doggerel and quickly turned my mind to *The Fantastic Four* and my new white German Shepherd.

Months later, in the mail, arrived this letter from some official-sounding state organization—the name is long forgotten; it was something like the North Carolina Department of Education's Elementary Library Association—informing me that some august strangers in Raleigh had read my fledgling work and had deemed it worthy of recognition. The title of the poem was mentioned in the body of the letter. Look at that! And I was hooked.

I'm sure the writers included in this excellent new volume, *Racing Home*, have similar stories to tell, some moment of their first validation outside of themselves. But one thing is certain: before they received that nod, that pat on the back, they first put words down on paper. Why do we do that? What impels us to write? And why do so many North Carolinian folk do it in comparison to other Americans? Surely we've recognized that something about the process itself satisfies the soul, just like reading good writing. It's kin to gossip, and step-father to the lie; it goes down like good wine and smells like sex; it can make you cry, laugh, sing, sweat and fall in love; it's ancient and fresh, simple and complex, solitary and communal.

The Old North State is world famous for producing writers. It is a mystery and a source of pride that we bring up so many, like tobacco plants from the soil. It is a tradition that began long before Thomas Wolfe and that continues well past Charles Kuralt. They spring up in the east (Charles Chestnutt), in the west (Wilma Dykeman), and in the middle (Doris Betts). They come schooled and unschooled, young and old. They win Pulitzer Prizes and National Book Awards, have movies and television shows based on their work, become best-selling phenomena, win the imprimatur of the Oprah-machine. This achievement from an overwhelmingly rural state with one of the most conservative senators (and one of the most liberal governors), with more hogs than people, and where the largest city resembles one gigantic Mayberry. Few states have approached North Carolina's obsession and exaltation and appreciation of writers. How many states can boast so many *intimately* beloved writers? By intimate, I mean to suggest writers whose books are anticipated and read; whose readings are supported; and whose names are often on folks' lips; truly beloved. Can you imagine John Updike evoking in the suburbs of Massachusetts and Connecticut the emotion that Clyde Edgerton inspires in downtown Laurinburg or Greensboro? I suspect that North Carolina's diligent readers, organizations like the North Carolina Writer's Network, active book clubs (long before they became a national trend), dedicated university and college writing programs, publishing companies like Algonquin and The Paper Journey Press, good bookstores, and good, word-struck, under-appreciated, hard-working elementary and high school teachers, help encourage and engender courage in our writers...perhaps. Or maybe it's just in the red clay and the swamps and the hollers.

Now here's an amazing thing about this collection: I consider myself fairly well-read, and up-to-date about my North Carolina writers, but I'm embarrassed to say I had not heard of one of the writers included here. That's not a bad thing. We are always looking for fresh new voices, and, even more importantly, we always want to know that there are exciting new writers on the horizon. These folk all write like Archangels with Avenging Pens. More than continuing the legacy of North Carolina writing, these writers are expanding the expectations of the new New New South. Geographically their stories range far and wide: from North Carolina to New York state to New Orleans to Durango, Colorado to the Mayo Clinic. Their subject matter is at once that of the human heart and of Stuff of the Now: car racing, television production, rock music, electro-shock treatments. No doubt we'll be hearing a great deal from these storytellers.

For whatever reason, we can rest assured that our state-wide flood of words continues to gush in this cell-phoned, jet planed, faxed, sonogrammed, interneted, CD-ROMed, gigabyte age. Whether we're drinking designer water or sweet ice tea, cappuccino or moonshine, eating sautéed chicken breast or fried chicken wings, caviar or chitlins – it seems the central itch, that desire to get it down, to get it down right, to write, continues on, propelled by I-don't-know-what, but it continues to gnaw at our souls and keep us writing. We North Carolinians continue to pick up the pen — or turn on the computer — and communicate. *Can I get an Amen?*

...There's something I just have to tell you... Did you hear?... Now, somebody told me...

Randall Kenan, 2001

stories

Background

Luke Whisnant

Saturday night, the Stones are tearing down the stadium across town. In comes Connor, carrying sound, and his cameraman, Skeeter, humping the NewsCenter 9 minicam and the shoulder pack. Connor one-eighties the jammed nightclub and notes a good mix of heads, a late-twenties to mid-thirties crowd: some nose-rings, some surfer dudes, lots of big-haired babes and punks in combat boots and buttoned-down corporate types, and a pack or two of Joe-Blow beer-commercial boy-next-doors. "Fertile ground here," he decides. Skeeter hoists the camera to his shoulder. "Cool," he says. "Let's deploy," he says, "let's rock and roll." They sidle into the crowd swirling four and five deep around the bar.

Q: What was the best concert you ever saw?
A: Soundgarden.
Q: What was the best concert you ever saw?
A: Springsteen. He kicked ass.
Q: What was the best concer—
A: Elvis.

Q: Elvis? You saw Elvis?
A: Naw. Not really. I was shittin' you. I just always wanted to see Elvis.

Skeet cuts the spot and turns toward the bar.

"Thanks for your time," Connor says.

Soundtrack: *Let It Bleed.* The overhead speakers kick and slam with the bass drum and Connor starts picking up distortion; he adjusts his levels. It occurs to him that Deever's crew would be backstage by now, shooting Mick Jagger from the wings, rubbing shoulders with roadies and groupies and maybe even interviewing Charlie or Keith or the singer in the opening band. He ought to be envious, but for some reason, he doesn't care. Summer doldrums, maybe—for weeks he's been on autopilot, just going through the motions.

Q: What was the best concert you ever saw?
A: Lollapalooza, man. By far.
Q: Why is that?
A: It was just, like, you know…Aww. You had to be there. I donno.
Q: What was the best concert you ever saw?
A: Okay, well, it would have been one of the Dead shows but I saw 'em like thirty-five or forty times so it's hard to say which one, you know?

Turning away, Connor murmers, "Hey, Skeet, know what a Deadhead says when he runs out of dope?…'Man, this music sucks.'"

"Yeah, I heard that one," Skeet says, grinning. "Freakin' Deadheads. Hey, how about the ancient mariner over in the corner?" He nods at an old man—down-turned mouth, wispy long white hair under a sailor cap—peering into a beer. "Do him," Skeet says. "For contrast."

"We'll get to him," Connor says.

Q: What was the best concert you ever saw?
A: Led Zeppelin, Detroit Coliseum, 1973.
Q: You don't look like a Zeppelin kinda guy.
A: Neither do you.
Q: I'm just curious. I think I saw that same tour. Do you remember what they opened with?
A: Yeah, "Black Dog." They were awesome. Enormous sound. Page was wearing his infamous dragon suit. Black silk bell-bottoms with a fire-breathing dragon embroidered up one leg, black silk jacket with a dragon across the shoulders. Whopping that sunburst Les Paul with a violin bow. What's this for?
Q: The news. How come you're not at the Stones concert tonight?
A: Oh, man, I'm all concerted-out.

"What's this for?" people always ask. "The news," Connor says, or sometimes he just points toward the minicam and Skeet half-turns so they can see the big red 9 and the LiveEye logo. People are confused, expecting the face reporters, anchors, the semifamous. Connor is a nobody. He rarely appears on camera. When asked, it pleases him to say that he makes his living in the shadows, lurking.

"Hey, newsdudes," somebody yells. "Newsdudes, hey. Film at eleven."

Q: What was the best concert you ever saw?
A: I never been to no concerts.
Q: You never been to a concert?
A: Fuck off, man.
Q: Sure thing. Nice talking to you, too... Hey, got a sec? What was the best concert you ever saw?
A: The Godfather of Soul, babe, the Numero Uno Sex Machine, I

mean—
gettin doooowwwn
wid Mista Jaaaames Brrooown.
Q: Uh huh. Well, thanks for your time.

"Change the question," Skeet says.

"Skeet," Connor says. "The question doesn't matter. You know that. It's all form, not content. We're just cooking up some eye candy here—pretty people and light and sound and the flickering electronic fireplace."

"What is with you lately, man?"

A decade ago, finishing up his Masters thesis in History, Connor would never have imagined himself in media—least of all television. He'd gotten in through a side door, though, during a local-market one-hour special on the fiftieth anniversary of the Great Depression Gaston Mill Riots; Connor had started out as a historical consultant and ended up co-producing. One thing had led to another; the field was overcrowded so he'd moved around a lot; and some days found him editing, some taking sound, some producing. Very rarely did he do a standup.

Q: What was the best concert you ever saw?
A: The Stones.
Q: The Rolling Stones?
A: The Rolling Stones, man. Greatest rock and roll band in the world.
Q: Why aren't you at the concert tonight?
A: Wasn't it sold out?
Q: No.
A: No?
Q: No. It's the first Stones show here not to sell out in 20 years.
A: Huh. Oh, well. Hey, you guys are Channel 9? I'm digging y'all's new Chinese anchor-girl.

Q: *Japanese.*
A: *Whatever. She's a babe-and-a-half.*
Q: *I'll tell her you said so.*
A: *Cool, man. Do. Darryl. Tell her Darryl said.*

"Tell her Skeet said, too," Skeet mutters, and Connor gives him a grin. "No comment," he says. He cups a hand over one ear, shoves the mike forward, yells.

Q: *What's the best concert you ever saw?*
A: *You're breathing my air.*
Q: *Pardon?*
A: *Later, man. Speak to the hand.*

She holds up her hand in a "halt" motion. Connor, despite himself, laughs. Never heard that one before.

Q: *What was the best concert you ever saw?*
A: *I would have to say ... John Pierre Rampal.*
Q: *Why?*
A: *What, aside from the fact that the man is a genius?*
Q: *Yes.*
A: *I'll tell you. See, it was Carnegie Hall, and the show sold out. They had sold too many tickets and there were about two dozen of us who didn't have seats. So they lined up some folding chairs for us on the stage, behind Rampal, and we watched the show sitting on the stage staring at Rampal's back, and everybody in the audience looking up at us.*
Q: *Is that right?*
A: *Sure. John Pierre Rampal Live at Carnegie Hall, on Columbia Masterworks—check out the cover photo next time you're in a record store. I'm right behind Rampal, third guy from the left. There's a woman in a purple dress on my left—my wife. She was just my*

girlfriend then.
A: Interesting. Okay, then — thanks for your time.

"Let's talk to some of these women, Skeet," Connor says. "And just for color, let's see if we can find a minority or two lurking about. But first, the women."

"I like blondes," Skeet tells him.

"That's a fun-fact I've never heard before," Connor says. "That's news to me."

"Kiss my ass," Skeet says, laughing.

Q: Hi, ladies. Be on TV, be famous for fifteen minutes. What was the best concert you ever saw?
A: Uh…let me think a sec.
Q: No thinking. Thinking's not allowed. It's TV. It's ephemeral. It disappears into thin air.
A: It does?
A: What a ditz. Don't interview her. Do me.
A: Shut up. He asked me first.
A: Jeeze. You'll just embarrass yourself, Angie.
Q: Thanks for your time.
A: Hey, wait a minute!
Q: Hello…What was the best concert you ever saw?
A: The one you're taking me to tomorrow night.
Q: Excuse me?

She stands there a moment, a vacuous look on her face, and then bursts into giggles. Connor, flummoxed, turns away awkwardly.

"Losing your edge," Skeet kids him.

"I'm out of practice," Connor agrees. "I admit it."

"When were you ever in practice?"

Connor essays an exaggerated and mock-mournful shrug.

A woman down the bar catches his eye. She's wearing a brown crop-top, black tights, and black ankle-boots, sitting with her legs crossed above the knee, her front foot kicking slightly in time with the music. Her dark hair is down, framing her face, and she watches him with smoky gray-green eyes as he slides toward her, Skeet following.

Q: Hi.
A: Hi.
Q: David Connor, NewsCenter 9.
A: Is that your real name? Connor?
Q: Yeah, why?
A: I thought all you TV people had fake names.
Q: Just the faces, not us grunts. I didn't catch your name.
A: It's Melissa. Think we could we do without the camera?
Q: We could, but then you'd miss your fifteen minutes of fame. What was the best concert you ever saw?
A: I'd rather not say.
Q: Why not?
A: It's not for public consumption. It's off the record. What do you guys call it? Background? Yeah, it's deep background.

Connor turns and looks at Skeet, eyebrows raised. Skeet cuts the spot, shaking his head. "Excuse us a minute," Connor says to Melissa.

He steers Skeet a few steps away, one hand on his shoulder, and bends toward his ear. "Let's call it a wrap, Skeeter," he says. "We've got plenty."

"Plenty of nothing," Skeet says, but he begins to unstrap the minicam.

"It's fluff," Connor says. "All they need is fifteen, twenty seconds." He glances at the Miller Time clock: 10:02. "You've got an hour 'til broadcast. They'll use it as the kicker, so say an hour-twenty 'til they roll it. Plenty of time for Jeanne to cob something together."

Skeet looks at him disgustedly. "You bailing, boss?"

Connor only winks.

* * *

When he saunters back in from helping Skeeter load the van, he finds Melissa has saved him a seat at the bar. She smiles at him, a little uneasily, he thinks; there's a dour air about her, guardedness, something he can't quite articulate. Recently single, Connor decides not to be too hopeful. Go with the flow, he reminds himself, and he orders a beer from the swamped bartender. Melissa says she's never seen it so crowded here. Connor tells her he doesn't get out much. He squints at the roils of slow-motion smoke against the faux-tile ceiling and hums along with the cranked sound system. "Sway" from *Sticky Fingers*.

"One of my favorite Stones songs," he explains.

"I can't get past the phrase 'evil life,'" Melissa tells him. "To me that's an oxymoron."

Connor tries to figure this out. Maybe she means palindrome, he thinks, but that doesn't quite add up either. Her eyes are uncommonly green—he suspects tinted contacts—and her gaze is steady, almost uncomfortably so. He avoids staring back; he glances at her amber earrings, her subtle brown-tinged lipstick, her short unpainted nails. She's drinking mineral water with a lime wedge. When she sets the glass back in the precise center of her napkin, he notices a dark smudge—a tattoo, a black pictograph—on the inside of her wrist.

"Is that kanji?" he asks.

She holds it up for him to examine. "Kanji is Japanese, right?"

Connor nods.

"This is Chinese."

"What does it mean?"

"I don't want to tell you."

"Why not?"

"I just don't."

"We're on background here, remember? No camera, no mike."

She sips from her water and Connor watches the lime wedge bump her brown lip. "Truth," she tells him. "It says Truth."

"Ah," Connor says.

"There was a time, not all that long ago, when I saw myself as a seeker of truth," she explains.

"Didn't we all," Connor says. He's surprised at how wistful he sounds.

"No. We all didn't. And those of us who did were just naïve." She rubs her thumb slowly over the black tattoo, as if to smear it. "Anyway, I'm saving up now to have it removed."

"Don't do anything rash," Connor says, smiling. "These things go in cycles. You never know when truth will be back in vogue. Isn't that right, Howie?" he asks the bartender.

Howie smiles politely, setting a napkin, a mug, and a fresh bottle of Amstel on the bar in front of Connor.

"See, this is why I didn't want to tell you. You think Truth is just some fad, like backgammon or Mayan astrology. But it's not."

"No, it's not," Connor agrees. "But what you're talking about, Truth with a capital T, that's the kind of truth most people are agnostics about."

"If they are, it's your fault. You and people like you."

Connor looks at her, eyebrows raised. Here it comes, he thinks.

"You go out into the world, you ask some questions, you get some answers, it doesn't matter if they're true or not, you throw them up on a TV screen and pretty soon nobody knows lies from truth, or gives a damn, either."

"That's different," Connor says. "That's TV truth."

It was incredible, he thought, how many times he had heard some variation of her accusation. He had evolved several defenses, one of which was a kind of ironic agreement, trotting hand-in-hand down the same path, nodding and smiling and admitting culpability in a voice so insincere that his attacker was often stopped short. Other times he would simply dismiss the argument out of hand—"You simply don't know what you're talking about," he'd say calmly, because usually, they didn't; they were outside peering in, they saw everything in black and white. Every now and then, though, he'd meet someone who he thought deserved to hear his side of it, and now Melissa strikes him as one of these. "TV truth," he explains, "is relative. It's context-based." It's all point of view and tone of voice and angle and setup, he tells her; it's all in the editing; it's sleight-of-hand, fix-it-in-the-mix; TV is the lie that helps you see the truth. "There are ten thousand masks on the face of truth," Connor says, "and we bring them to you, every single face, two dozen at a time." It was art. That was the bottom line. Everything is true, everything. He tells her he cannot think of one false thing that isn't also true.

"You really believe that?" Melissa asks.

"You can't step in the same river twice," Connor says, miming a flowing river with his extended hand.

"What the hell does that mean?"

"It means that truth is flux. It's always changing. Every time you go back to that same place in the river, it's new water under your foot."

"Truth is not a river," she says. "We're talking about two entirely different things."

"Look, I'll give you an example," he says. "I'm interviewing this guy tonight who tells me he was onstage with Jean Pierre Rampal, that he's on the album cover. Now strictly speaking—"

"Stop," she says. "Please. I don't want to hear it."

For some reason she seems to be close to tears. Connor, surprised, realizes he has not been paying attention. He cannot think how to get back to square one. He touches her arm. She recoils, sliding off her barstool out of his reach.

"I thought you were someone else," she explains.

"Pardon?"

"It's just that you look very much like this guy I knew," she says in a rush. "Plus he worked for a TV station or a radio station or something like that." She looks into his eyes one at a time, right then left then right again, as if trying to read his thoughts. "He had some fucked-up ideas about truth, too, let me tell you."

In the sudden silence between songs she drops a five on the bar and spins off through the crowd. Connor watches her all the way to the door, willing her to turn back and meet his gaze. She doesn't.

*   *   *

"I was trying to warn you," Howie says. "I was trying to shoot you the high sign over here."

"What high sign?"

Howie twirls his index finger in small circles at his forehead.

"That's not the high sign," Connor says.

"Whatever."

"You think she's crazy, Howie?"

"Well, duh," Howie says. "She gives you all that crap about TV is the Great Satan, but I tell you what—right now she's racing home in her little red Miata trying to catch her five-second cameo on the eleven o'clock."

"Maybe she wants to tape it for her mama," Connor says. "That doesn't make her crazy."

Howie shakes his head. "Connor, another minute and she'd have slapped your face. And for what? I'm telling you, man, I know this chick, and she's loony tunes."

Connor watches him wipe the spotless bar with a white cloth.

"She's not crazy," he says. "She just had me mixed up with someone else."

Her mistaken recognition weighs oddly on him. Not long ago on the courthouse sidewalk a persistent and maniacal bag lady had proclaimed him to be Jesus, had sworn she had seen him heal the blind. Connor had corrected her, had told her his name, had gone so far as to show her his unscarred palms. The old lady, betrayed, bitterly told him to forget it, but the encounter had haunted him; he had a sense that he'd misunderstood, that it was all metaphor, and perhaps he was oblivious to his own Christ-nature. This deal tonight had had the same quality, he thinks, a weird, addled kind of logic. For if what he believed was right—that everything was true—then maybe he was who she'd mistaken him for. No, he thinks, she's not crazy.

When the news comes on, he leaves his stool and stands as close to the TV as he can and motions to Howie to turn it up. The old man in the sailor cap—Skeeter's ancient mariner—mutters something unhappy into his beer and fixes him with baleful eye. Connor ignores him. He notes that Annette has put her hair back since the six-o'clock, and John has changed his tie. Otherwise, the broadcast is oddly the same, as if nothing new has happened in the past five hours. Connor finds himself sketching pretend Chinese pictograms on a bar napkin. When Deever's report on the Stones concert comes up—live from the stadium, show still in progress—he barely glances at it.

"Looks like maybe they won't get to your stuff," Howie says, nodding at the clock.

"Don't jinx it."

At 11:24, Annette smiles at the camera and says, "And finally tonight, we asked some folks who didn't make it to the Stones show what their favorite concert was. Here are some of their answers."

Connor braces himself, leans forward against the bar.

Cut to crowd scene in bar. Camera pans.

Cut to stoner girl, dreadlocks and tank top: "Soundgarden."

Cut to guy in tie and button-down: "Led Zeppelin."

Cut to bearded man: "Elvis."

Cut to Howie, popping the top on a beer bottle, smiling.

Cut to man in sweater: "I would have to say...Jean-Pierre Rampal."

Cut to Darryl: "The Rolling Stones, man. Greatest rock and roll band in the world."

Annette, laughing, voice over: "You have to wonder why he wasn't at the show."

Cut to the speak-to-the-hand woman holding up her hand; John, voice-over: "I was just thinking that myself...So, Annette, what was your favorite concert?"

Cut back to studio. Annette, looking dreamily at John, says, "Michael Bolton."

Connor wrinkles his face. Howie laughs. "I was digging her until right then," he explains.

"Pink Floyd," John is saying. "Absolutely tra nscendental."

"He was tripping," Connor says. He finds himself unaccountably disgusted; he wonders if he's drunk. "Turn it off, Howie."

Heading out, he passes the old sailor, on his way back from the men's room. Connor grabs hold of his shoulder and asks if he has a favorite concert. The old man shakes his head, but to Connor it seems he is negating the question, not answering it. "What is Truth?" Connor asks. "Do you know? Isn't everything true?"

"I got no time for your foolishness," the old man says.

The End of Hemingway

Ellen Devlin

On Saturday night, July 1, 1961, at 8:35 in the evening, Bobby Rilliard had a car wreck on Old Post Road in Dobbs Ferry, New York.

Though it had rained earlier that night and the road was moist, it was not raining anymore when Bobby left the Tarrytown Tavern at 8:15. In fact, some stars were beginning to twinkle through the veil that wafted across the night sky. Before climbing in behind the wheel, Bobby had cranked all the car windows wide open, "just like in a convertible." He wanted the rush of fresh air to keep him awake over the drumbeat of the ten beers he'd drunk in his two hours of taverning. He was going to be alert.

But despite all his efforts, and for no reason at all, really, the front wheels of the two-toned lime-green '59 Plymouth four-door sedan he was driving turned with murderous precision to the left. Poor Bobby was happily humming along to an Everly Brothers tune on the radio, going about 45 miles per hour, unmindful of the mechanical mutiny that was taking place a mere three feet from his toes. Insidiously, the Plymouth's tires rotated slightly due east on the oozy asphalt of Old Post Road until its sharp hood ornament began seeking out the blurring trees and thickets lining the far shoulder. Bobby's hands and forearms were pleasantly numb, and his eyes were lolling over to the west, dreamily trying to glimpse the sky over the Hudson River as he drove south to Dobbs Ferry. Wasn't there supposed to be a full moon tonight?

If Bobby Rilliard had departed the Tarrytown Tavern five minutes earlier than he did, or five minutes later—hell, if he'd left 30 seconds sooner or later—the young woman in the other car would not have endured such a gruesome end. Both cars would have missed each other—passing with a wet, whispering hiss—to vanish forever on that black road so long ago.

But that's not the way it happened.

On a gentle blind turn, the car Bobby was driving sliced slowly across the northbound lane of Old Post Road. That's where the new 1961 Oldsmobile, black, four-door sedan, speeding around the turn at 60 miles per hour, plowed mightily into the Plymouth's right front grille.

There was a short screech, then an explosion like cannon shot as the two cars—for one thunderous moment—became one. The giant hulks shuddered at impact, their rear axles rising off the ground. Then the cars parted and squealed into slow half-circles before coming to rest in an angry fountain of sparks in the center of the road.

The front-seat passenger in the Olds, a 24-year-old woman, was ejected through the windshield in a comet of glass. She skimmed the hood for only a split second. Then, horribly, she came to ground in the muddy ditch that ran beside the roadway.

Someone once said that we all owe God a death, and so the young woman settled her debt early and horribly in a sluice of mud and sticks after only a gasp of surprise.

The top of her head had been sheared completely off, leaving nothing but a cap of pink and gray coils where her carefully curled blonde hair had once been. Bright hot blood—pumping from a heart that hadn't yet learned of her death—sent gouts of red seeping along the seams of her gray summer dress and puddling onto the rocks that ringed her head. The driver of the Olds, the steering column jammed against his sternum, sat stone-still in his seat, his head thrown forward by the impact. He was unconscious. But he would live. In a manner of speaking, he would live, but he would never speak again.

Of course, Bobby didn't know about the death. Or the injury. What little attention he retained—after he'd struggled back up behind the steering wheel from off the floorboards and began looking around—was riveted on the Oldsmobile parked at a drunken angle across the road. All he could see was the shadow of the other driver behind the steering wheel. The shadow never moved at all.

Fuck! What happened?

All Bobby Rilliard knew for certain was that he was in a universe of trouble. After all, the Plymouth wasn't even his. It belonged to his drinking buddy, Emmett O'Malley of Yonkers.

* * *

At 9:10 the same evening, the phone rang and frightened twelve-year-old Maeve O'Malley off of her seat. She had been perched on a stool at the bar in the rec room basement of the O'Malley's rented house. She was watching the second rerun of *The Day the Earth Stood Still* on the 14" black-and-white television set mounted over the bar. The phone rang again.

Oh, hell! she thought. *Go away! This is the best part. Almost.* She edged back onto the barstool.

The telephone called to her a third time.

Maeve, her attention glued to the television screen, was willing to let the phone keep ringing. But then a sobering thought occurred to her. It just might be her parents calling, checking up on her. Maeve's parents, Emmett O'Malley and his wife Eileen, were not home. It was Saturday night. The O'Malleys had gone out drinking with their friends Ida and Lefty in the little bar at the foot of Glenwood Avenue, just a few blocks away. They had dictated to Maeve a strict set of protocols before they left; if she did not act responsibly and behave herself when home alone, she would never be allowed to watch *Saturday Night at the Movies* ever again.

Maeve O'Malley stepped quickly to the telephone while glancing over her shoulder, squinting at the television screen as she went. Any second now, the magnificent Michael Rennie— in his role as Klattoo the Spaceman—would emerge from his flying saucer and pour his honeyed voice into the room.

Maeve's heart hammered as she picked up the phone.

"Hello?"

"Yes. Hello. Is this the O'Malley residence?" a deep male voice inquired. There was a hint of New York in his voice. Just a hint.

"Yes? I mean, yes," Maeve answered, panting a little bit. "It is."

"Is Mr. or Mrs. O'Malley at home?"

"Uh, no. They…they're out. For a little while. They're at the bar down on Glenwood."

"May I ask to whom I'm speaking?"

"Wha—uh, this is their daughter. Maeve."

"May I ask how old you are?"

"I'm twelve. I just turned twelve in June."

There was a scratchy pause on the line, as if the caller were debating something. Then,

"Okay, miss?"

"Yes?"

"I'm going to ask you to do something very, very important."

"Okay."

"Are you listening?"

"Yeah?"

"This is the Dobbs Ferry Police Department."

"Uh-huh."

"There's been an accident with your father's car and we need to talk to him right away. Can you get him for us? This is very, very important."

Maeve O'Malley, her pigtails flying, her flip-flops flapping, ran down the hill to the little tavern where her parents were drinking. She pushed her way through the smudged glass door and into the dark, smoky room. A jukebox, arched with bright neon tubing, played jazz tunes loudly in the corner. Dark forms milled about, laughing and talking. The ceiling of the place seemed to rise up and up forever, it being invisible in the hazy dark. Maeve had no trouble spotting the hulk of her father, his back to the door, leaning at the bar. In profile, his broken nose gave him the belligerent air of a prizefighter, even when he smiled. He was talking very closely, intimately, to his friend Lefty. Maeve couldn't spot her mother anywhere.

Squirming between the clots of people, Maeve reached her father and tapped him on the back. Twice. Emmett O'Malley finally turned his big smiling head around and stared down at her. Once their eyes locked, his smile froze into a sort of rictus. He stared down at his skinny little daughter, with her scraped knees peaking beneath the hems of her baggy orange shorts.

"What the hell are *you* doing here?" he demanded.

* * *

Maeve O'Malley sat scrunched halfway down the basement steps, listening pale and round-eyed as her parents argued back and forth in the kitchen.

"Emm, I told you that this would happen! Didn't I?

Didn't—"

"God*damn* it, Eileen! Would you stop flogging me? This is not the time or—"

"What did you expect? Like this is such a big news flash? You let that *sot* drive around in our car? Did you think he was going to use it to drive to a church picnic?! What if he's killed somebody?"

"He hasn't killed anybody, for Chrissakes. Now, stop being hysterical."

"I'm not hysterical!"

"Until we find out what happened, we're not going to play war games about it! It's probably nothing…"

"With Bobby Rilliard, *nothing* is nothing!"

Neither Eileen nor Emmett knew Maeve was sitting down there. They thought she'd descended into the basement to watch the rest of the movie while Emmett began pawing at the wall phone. Emmett was drunk, but not drunk enough that somebody who didn't know him would notice. His words slurred only a little bit as he had ordered Maeve away.

"But Daddy, what'll we *do?*"

"*You're* not going to do a goddamn thing except go downstairs and watch the idiot box while I take care of this! Now get the hell out of here!" Emmett O'Malley had yelled this as he patted his shirt pocket for the pack of Pall Malls he kept there.

Maeve O'Malley had crept halfway down the stairs and then stopped when she heard her father speaking into the phone. She was more than willing to forego the end of *The Day the Earth Stood Still* in order to witness this horrible new drama. She sat down.

As she sat still as death on that step, listening, she realized that a strange twist coiled this new plot.

Emmett O'Malley was not calling the Dobbs Ferry Police Department as she thought he would. Strange. He was, instead, calling his friend John Krackowsky, who lived in Dobbs Ferry.

John Krackowsky, Maeve knew, was a Dobbs Ferry policeman. He was off-duty that Saturday night, and didn't know anything about what had happened on the wet road. But he had a police scanner in his home, and Maeve heard her father ask him to consult it. After about a million minutes, Maeve then heard Emmett O'Malley pleading with his friend over the telephone.

"Jesus Christ, John! This is a friggin' *disaster*! We could be *sued* over this! Our insurance company won't even *touch* this! I know. What? I *know that*, but I didn't think that moron would do—what? Aw, *shit*! No. No, I didn't. The kid talked to 'em. Why? Oh, Jesus. Didn't think of it. All right. All right. I'll talk to her and then I'll call you right back."

Talk to *her*? *Which* her? *Her-Maeve*? *Why*?

As Emmett slammed the phone down on its hook, Maeve O'Malley quickly descended to the foot of the stairs, biting her lower lip as she went. Hurry. *Hurry*! When she reached the bottom, she lingered there behind the thick wooden post, waiting for the summons from above.

"Maeve! *Maeve!*" The voice was like thunder coming down from the ceiling.

"Uh, yeah?" Maeve called up the stairs.

"Maeve, get up here. I wanna to talk to you."

Jesus.

Maeve slowly ascended the basement steps and then rounded the corner into the kitchen. Her mother Eileen sat at the Formica kitchen table, looking down at her hands folded carefully on the table before her. Eileen had kept her red hair long in those days, and several neon strands escaped from the coil of her French twist and snaked down the sides of her neck. There was a dark scrim of sweat at the neckline of her green cotton dress. Just above the edge of the neckline, Eileen's red freckles pulsated on her throat. Her face was still flushed from the argument.

Maeve's father paced back and forth across the squeaky kitchen floor between the table and the stove, smoking as he went. His plaid cotton shirt was open at the neck, and its tail hung out from his pants in the back. His belly bulged damply over his belt. When he caught sight of Maeve standing at the doorway, he stopped his walk and stared at her. The overhead kitchen light seemed to make his crooked nose—smashed sometime during the war—seem even more deviant than it actually was. Even from where she stood, even over the swirl of cigarette smoke, Maeve could smell her father's sweat and the beer he had drunk.

"Maeve, c'mere!" her father ordered. "C'mere and sittdown." He pointed with his chin to the vacant chair that stood opposite Eileen. Maeve O'Malley silently obeyed. As soon as she sat, Emmett O'Malley crouched down on the floor before her.

"Now, Maeve," he began. "I want you to listen very carefully. Are you listening?" The beer smell was much stronger now, but Maeve dare not turn her face away. Not now. She couldn't bear to look her father in his green eyes, and concentrated instead on the speck of white spittle caked in the corner of his mouth.

"Yeah?" she said.

"Now, you remember when the Dobbs Ferry Police called here tonight?"

Maeve nodded. Of *course* she remembered! Did he think she was a complete idiot?

"Now, I want you to think very, very carefully. I want you to remember everything you told the cops. Do you think you can do that?" Under the tangle of dark brown hair, Emmett O'Malley's forehead was pearly with sweat. "Every word. Can you do that?"

Maeve nodded. Perhaps desperately. What would happen to her if she couldn't remember every single word that was said?

"Did you tell the cops that I loaned Uncle Bobby the car tonight?"

"What…our car?"

Emmett grimaced, squeezed his eyes shut, and rubbed his forehead in frustration.

"Mother of Jesus," he muttered. Then he opened his eyes wide and snarled, "No, I meant President Kennedy's limousine. YES, OUR CAR! Whose car didja think, Maeve?"

"I–I don't know, Daddy." Maeve's lower lip began to quiver.

"All right, all right. I'm sorry. Yes, our car. Now, think. Didja tell the cops I loaned it to Uncle Bobby?"

Maeve O'Malley, sitting there benumbed, performed a crystal-sharp scan of her thoughts, her memory, her entire consciousness. Her search was cosmic in its scope and intensity. Her eyeballs jittered in their sockets as she scanned invisible parchments in the air. Emmett spoke again.

"Now, it's okay if you *did* tell them that I loaned Bobby the car," Emmett continued, but Maeve knew that it was most definitely *not* okay to have told them that. Not at all. "After all," Emmett continued, "you didn't know any better. Right? But I need to know if you told them that I loaned Uncle Bobby the car. It's important."

Maeve O'Malley closed her eyes and concentrated. The seconds ticked their deadly progression into the night. She could hear and smell her father's every breath as she pondered. Finally, she opened her eyes and spoke.

"No."

"No what?"

"I didn't mention anybody loaning anything."

"You swear to *Christ* you didn't mention that?"

"Dad! All I said was that you and mom were drinking at the bar—"

"*Shit!*" Her father's whole face winced in anger and pain.

Maeve could feel her eyes rounding in a new panic. Then her father spoke quickly again.

"Okay, okay! That's not the issue here. Do you remember telling them *anything* about me loaning *anything* to *anybody?*"

"*No!* The man said there was an accident with the car, and could he talk to you or Mom, and I said you weren't here, that you and Mom were at the-at-the-at-the b-b-bar, and then he said can you get them, and then I said I would, and then I hung up and ran to get you."

Maeve's intake of breath after that seemed to suck the room empty.

"You swear to Christ that's all you said?"

Maeve nodded solemnly. That was indeed all that she had said.

Emmett O'Malley lumbered to his feet and then emitted a cavernous sigh.

"Thank Christ," he said. "Thank Christ!" He put his cigarette down in the ashtray and rubbed his mouth with the back of his hand.

Then he banished Maeve to the underworld once again.

"Okay. Okay. Now go finish watching your movie."

Maeve O'Malley, thankful that she'd escaped vengeance so easily, arose from her seat, tiptoed down the stairs, and fairly skipped across the black and white tiles to the bar and the television set. She settled down on the barstool, leaned her elbows on the bar, and returned to a parallel universe and the drama concluding there.

* * *

Mid-morning on Sunday, Maeve O'Malley arose from her bed and, in her pajamas, shuffled into the kitchen. Sunday mornings meant pancakes, and Maeve delighted in her job as batter mixer. She looked forward to stirring up the buckwheat batter, adding milk and eggs just as the recipe on the box had commanded. Maeve's parents usually never got up until after 11 o'clock on Sunday mornings, so Maeve had this process all to herself. Emmett and Eileen were usually never around on Sunday mornings to scold her for licking the spoon and the bowl clean when she was finished with her cooking.

However, on that gray Sunday, Maeve was surprised and more than a bit disappointed to see both parents in the kitchen. Both of them. Eileen O'Malley was standing at the counter, her back to the doorway, vigorously stirring the contents of the big blue bowl. Emmett was hunched at the table in his navy blue terrycloth bathrobe, smoking a cigarette and slowly turning a cup of coffee around and around in its saucer. The dark circles beneath Emmett's green eyes announced the sort of night he'd had.

The radio was playing.

Eileen O'Malley summoned Maeve to the table to eat. Two empty plates, sticky with syrup, crossed with cutlery, told her that her parents had already eaten. It was she, Maeve, who had slept late.

As Eileen brought Maeve's plate to her, Emmett rose from his chair and announced that he was going to take a shower. His friend Lefty was coming by in an hour to give him a lift to Dobbs Ferry. To straighten something out. To file a report. As Maeve brought her glass of orange juice up to her lips, Emmett snubbed out his cigarette in the sticky pool of syrup on his plate, got up and left the kitchen.

Only after Emmett left, did Maeve summon up the courage to ask Eileen about the trouble of the night before.

"What happened with the accident? You know. Last night."

"He's in jail," her mother said.

"Who's in jail?"

"Bobby. Bobby Rilliard. He's in jail. The jerk."

"Why's he in jail?"

"For getting in the accident." Eileen seemed darkly annoyed by something yet unspoken hanging in the air.

"Oh."

Eileen O'Malley poured herself a cup of black coffee and sat down. She was wearing her favorite yellow shirtwaist dress, neatly starched and pressed. However, Eileen's face in the gray light of the morning was drawn and tired. Her coppery hair hung down over her shoulders. She had not yet brushed the snarls from it.

"When's Uncle Bobby getting out of jail?" Maeve asked. She began shaving little yellow curls of butter from the stick in the blue-rimmed saucer to put on her pancakes.

Eileen's retort, sharp as a gunshot, stung the air.

"Don't call him 'Uncle Bobby' anymore! He's not your uncle. Never was!"

"Oh," Maeve said quietly.

Eileen immediately repented.

"I'm sorry, honey. It's not your fault. Bobby's caused us a lot of trouble lately, is all. Please, just don't call him 'Uncle' anymore. Okay?"

"Okay. So…when's…Bobby getting out of jail?"

"Never, I hope."

"Well, why not? It was an accident, wasn't it? He didn't do it on *purpose*, did he?"

"No. He didn't do it on purpose. Not the accident, anyway. It was the car. He…took Daddy's car. He…he…stole Daddy's car."

Maeve put the knife down on the saucer that cradled the butter.

"What? He *stole* it? I thought that—"

"Maeve, listen. There are many things that you don't understand yet. What happened last night was nasty and awful, but it's over and done with, and we won't talk about this again. Ever. We'll take care of it. You understand?"

Maeve nodded.

"That means you don't talk about this at school. You hear me?"

Maeve nodded.

"You don't know all the details, and you shouldn't talk about anything you know nothing about. As far as you're concerned, it never happened. Do you understand?"

Maeve nodded.

"Remember, if you talk about it, we'll know. Maybe not right away, maybe not next week, but we'll find out sooner or later. You understand?"

Maeve nodded.

Eileen picked up her cup and sipped at its steamy contents. "The jerk," she muttered between sips.

The radio brought the news just as Emmett O'Malley returned—shaven and combed and dressed—into the kitchen. Eileen, her eyes the size of biscuits, called "hush-hush" to the whole room as soon as a certain name was uttered over the air.

Ernest Hemingway.

Emmett O'Malley's face flushed, then paled as he stood transfixed, listening to the broadcast. A writer named Ernest Hemingway had apparently committed suicide in a place called Ketchum, Idaho in the early hours of the morning. The writer had been in failing health for a number of years. He'd won the Pulitzer Prize and the Nobel Prize for literature. Hemingway had been wounded as an ambulance driver in World War I, and had been a war correspondent in World War II. Five of his works had been made into films. In a few weeks, he would have been 62 years old.

When the short broadcast ended and the music began playing again, Emmett O'Malley spoke to the kitchen. His mouth drew into a satisfied grimace as he spoke.

"Well, you can't say this weekend was a *complete* wash," he muttered. "'We all owe God a death.' Ha. Isn't that what that coward once said? 'Apparent suicide.' Yeah, right. Apparent, my ass. That coward cashed in his own chips today, didn't he? This is the best news I've heard all day. All *week*!"

"Emmett—"

"Son of a bitch finally punched his own ticket. Couldn't take it on the chin, could he? Could dish it out, but couldn't take it."

"Emm, I think Lefty's outside waiting for you," Eileen announced into her cup. But her husband was still mired in his dark reverie.

"Yep. Took the coward's way out. It figures. Whatya expect from a man who throws sucker punches at you when your back is turned? Well, good riddance to that overrated asshole."

"Emm. Lefty. All right?"

Emmett O'Malley silently shook his head as he studied his shoes for a minute. Then he reached back to check his rear pants pocket for his wallet, and took his leave. His friend Lefty was indeed sitting in a car at the curb, waiting to drive him to Dobbs Ferry. Waiting to straighten something out.

When the screen door of the kitchen banged shut, Maeve O'Malley asked her mother another question.

"Who was Ernest Hemingway?"

"A writer. Wrote novels."

"Why did he kill himself?"

Eileen O'Malley heaved a sigh of exasperation.

"Maeve, how should *I* know? I never met the man. Daddy knew him." As soon as the words escaped her pale mouth, the flushed expression on Eileen O'Malley's face told Maeve that she repented them.

"Daddy knew this guy? They were friends?"

"Oh-no," Eileen said quietly. There was a dip of resignation in her voice. Then, a slight titter behind lips pressed firmly together. She spoke again. "No. They were most definitely *not* friends. Daddy and Ernest Hemingway got into a fight once in Cuba."

"Really? In Cuba?"

"Yeah. When Daddy was on leave there. In the Navy. It was in a bar in Havana. During the war."

"Well, why did they get into a fight?"

"Maeve, I have no idea. It was a long time ago. More than fifteen years now. It doesn't matter anymore. It was probably something stupid. As usual. Ha. I don't even believe that your *father* remembers now."

Maeve pondered on this for a moment. Distant fists and angry shouts swirled in a smoky corner of her mind. She could almost smell the beer and the acid scent of cigarettes. Then, a question presented itself.

"Who won the fight?" she asked, finally.

Eileen O'Malley was silent for a moment as the corners of her mouth turned in a tight little smile. Her face flushed pinker yet as she released a naughty little secret into the morning.

"Hemingway," she finally said. "Hemingway won. He was the one who broke Daddy's nose. He was twenty years older than your father, and really out of shape, but he won the fight anyhow."

"Wow. That's something. He just snuck up on Daddy while his back was turned. A...a...sneaky punch."

Then came Eileen's second little treachery of the day.

"Maeve. How can you punch somebody in the nose by sneaking up on him from behind? Hm? Think about it."

"Oh."

"You see. That's why we don't talk about it. Don't say a word about this to Daddy."

"Okay."

"And not in school, either."

"All right. I promise."

"Besides, nobody'll believe you anyway."

"I know," Maeve whispered. "I know."

* * *

Three years later, as Emmett O'Malley began his slow death from cirrhosis of the liver, fifteen-year-old Maeve O'Malley hurried to the Yonkers Public Library to check out a book she'd reserved there. It was the last book Hemingway ever wrote, and Maeve wanted to find out more about this man who had broken her father's nose. Maybe there was even a mention of that very fistfight in this very book! Not wanting anybody to see her with this book, Maeve carried it outside and sat down on a stone bench to peruse it. Thank God it was a slender volume that she could absorb in nearly one sitting, because she knew that she would never be able to bring this book home. *A Moveable Feast*, a memoir published posthumously in 1964.

But it was not about Cuba in the 1940s at all. It was about Ernest Hemingway's life in Paris, in the early 1920s. Way before the fistfight in question. Despite Maeve's initial disappointment, she settled down onto the shadowy stone bench and opened to the first page anyway. She waited hard for this book, and now she aimed to read it. The spring leaves rustled overhead, but soon she couldn't hear them at all. In no time, Maeve O'Malley was sitting in a café in Paris in 1922, and it was raining outside. The door of the café opened, and a young woman with a rain-freshened face entered and sat down at a table near the door. Her black hair formed a crow's wing across her cheek.

And Hemingway wrote that the young woman belonged to him now, and all Paris belonged to him now, and he belonged to his notebook and his pencil.

Maeve sat transfixed, reading page after page after page. In this book, Hemingway wrote of the fabulous meals in Paris bistros, and skiing trips to Shruns, Austria. There were literary discussions in the apartment of two lesbians, Gertrude Stein and Alice B. Toklas. There was the loony car trip with a writer named Fitzgerald, and drinks with the writer's crazy wife Zelda. And of course, Hemingway's confession about his betrayal of his first wife

Hadley; about how he wished he'd died before he'd ever loved anyone but her.

Maeve didn't realize how long she'd been sitting there, reading, until the light began to fail and she could no longer make out the words on the pages. But she'd gotten most of it, even if it meant she had to skip to the very end.

Then it was over. Maeve returned to Yonkers, saddened.

She stood up, walked to the library just as it was closing, and returned the book to the librarian.

"What? Finished already?" the lady asked.

"Yes." Maeve said. Then she was gone.

As the Hudson River swallowed up the dying sun, Maeve O'Malley was racing home. She wanted to get there first and hide herself in the sanctuary of the basement before the yellow-skinned Emmett returned from the tavern to read both their sins on her face.

Missing

Diana H. Renfro

I don't know why I decided to go. Lisa had been missing for two weeks and I'd begun to cave in, to think the worst. I wanted my wife back, or at the very least, just to know for sure that she was dead. Waiting was hell. So the same afternoon that Madge Blalock called, I left work to meet her. She had seen someone who looked a lot like Lisa on a bus to New Orleans the day she disappeared. Unlike most of the crackpots who'd been calling me, Madge Blalock sounded reasonable; her voice reminded me a little of my mother's. So this thin new strand of hope pulled me up and out to Madge Blalock's house to see what she was about.

It was early November, Thursday, and I agreed to meet at her house because she said a "passel of kids" would be in and out and she needed to be at home. Now I sat in her kitchen stirring the cup of coffee she'd given me, not asking if I wanted it but what I wanted in it, as a tall boy with braces ran through calling, "Hi, Mom," and tossing a book bag in a chair. He closed a door somewhere down a hallway and turned on some music.

It didn't seem to bother Madge that I was a stranger. She

talked to me as if she were quite used to having strays pull up to this yellow pine table to listen and drink coffee as she cooked dinner.

"I've been visiting my daughter Ellen in New Orleans," she began. "She has a brand new baby girl, Maggie. Isn't it amazing how fast you can fall in love with a baby?" Madge rinsed her hands in the sink and wiped them on a dishtowel. "I went down on the bus just to help Ellen a few days and ended up staying way too long."

My collar felt tight and I pulled on the knot of my tie to loosen it. The heat accumulating in the kitchen was making me sweat.

"My husband and the boys finally insisted it was time for me to come home. I got back yesterday. This morning I got out the newspapers B.G. stacked up for me while I was gone and tried to catch up on all the news. It was a bit overwhelming after two weeks. But I just started in the beginning, at the bottom of the stack. The only story I read was about your wife's disappearance. I was shocked when I saw her picture."

I cleared my throat to speak. "You've seen her?"

"She's the very person who sat beside me on the bus to New Orleans that day. I left Charlotte on Trailways at eleven."

My heart lurched forward, but I didn't want to get my hopes up again for nothing. "How sure are you?"

"Well, her hair was pulled back different from the picture. And she didn't smile at all. It's hard to be certain, but when I read that her husband's name was Frank, I decided to call you. That's too much of a coincidence. It has to be her and I hope for your sake, and especially for hers and the baby's, that you're the Frank she spoke about and you'll be able to trace her from there."

She must have seen the disappointment in my face. "What's the matter?"

"We don't have a baby." I swallowed hard. "Did she tell you

she had a baby?"

Her expression clouded and her eyes grew distant. I could almost see her thoughts pull inward behind her eyes. Turning away, she stirred some sautéing onions with a wooden spatula. Then she shifted back and looked right at me, her hands on her hips like a mother who thinks her kid is telling a lie. "You don't have a baby?"

I took a long breath. I didn't want to go into a lengthy explanation, so I simply said, "No, no children."

"Well, I guess that changes everything." Madge squinted as if remembering required more concentration now. "Her baby girl, Angela, was the whole reason for our quick friendship. I was on my way to meet my first granddaughter, you understand." She looked at me with sad eyes. "I'm really sorry. I must be all wrong about this."

"It's no problem," I said, standing to go. Hers wasn't the first false lead, but this one wrung me out. Never had it been so close. I wanted to go out and come back in, start over and get it right.

A timer went off and Madge opened the oven. She took out an iron skillet of crusty brown cornbread and closed it quickly to avoid the escaping heat. The kitchen door swung open behind her and a linebacker of a young man came in and kissed her on the cheek. "Yumm," he said, lingering over the stove moving his face from pan to steaming pan.

"Gerald, this is Mr. Frank Despin," she said, and to me, "This is my oldest son, Gerald, Jr."

He looked at me and put his hand straight out. "Pleased to meet you." He smiled handsomely. "Here for dinner?"

"No, I was…"

"Do stay for dinner," Madge said without hesitation. "It's the least I can offer after putting you through this."

"No. Thank you, but…"

"You have dinner plans already?"

"It's not that."

"Well then, stay. My other son and Big Gerald will be here within the hour, and the table's set. We'll just add another place. That's all there is to it."

"Give up, Mr. Despin. You can't argue with my mom about dinner."

"Well…" I wouldn't have argued with Gerald about anything. "If you're sure…"

"Good," said Madge. "Gerald, show him to a more comfortable place to sit and you two can get to know each other while you wait."

*　*　*

In the den, Gerald pointed to a sofa. "Where do you work?" he asked, switching on the television.

"I'm an accountant. With First Accounting, uptown."

"Oh yeah? I'm studying to be an accountant." His eagerness was tiresome. For a moment he watched the weatherman then he turned back to me. "I started a small business last year, landscaping, for neighbors mostly. I've had to invest in some big equipment and get some help." As another man entered the room, he stood and said, "Hi, Dad. Come meet Mr. Despin. He's with First Accounting."

"Well, I declare." The older man, whose size and appearance was nearly identical to the younger, thrust out a hand. "Gerald Blalock; B.G. for short."

He sat down across from me and Gerald said, "Dad, I was starting to tell him my experience with accounting." They shared a smile and Gerald looked back at me. "I've been doing my own books, but it's getting ahead of me. There's so much to keep up with. Especially the taxes."

They both looked at me then and waited. I sat in awkward silence, wondering what comment they expected.

"I'd…well, sure," I said after a moment. "I'd be happy to go over your records. Call my office tomorrow and set up a time."

"Great." He seemed satisfied and as the conversation lulled momentarily, we all turned to the television screen where a still photograph of a child was underlined with, "Have you seen me?" I thought of Lisa. Her picture had been on television like this for a week, requesting information surrounding her disappearance. Now, she'd been replaced.

Something plucked at my mind, like movement near the corner of my eye. I turned my head, but nothing was there. *What on earth am I doing here?* I stood up to go but Madge walked in calling us to dinner. Gerald and his father stood up too, smiling and commenting on my readiness, and I moved with the tide into the dining room and was cornered into a chair and there I sat.

From someplace within the house, Madge had gathered three sons whose appetite at the table reminded me of how I felt about my mother's meals at their age. The roast and rice with gravy looked and smelled like one of my mother's Sunday dinners. Hot cornbread, iced tea with lemon, green beans. Like B.G., my dad sat at the head of the table.

More introductions. The boy I'd seen earlier was Robert. Jake, younger, wanted to hear about New Orleans, and Eddie, four or five, focused intently on his mother's descriptions of his new niece.

"We'll see her Thanksgiving," said B.G., "and that won't be long."

"She won't be so tiny then," Madge told Eddie. "You can hold her."

"I wanna see her now," said Eddie. I knew the feeling, but something else was connecting in my mind about a baby — about the baby that actually disappeared around the same time Lisa did. As they talked, my achy emptiness filled with apprehension.

Eddie looked up at me and asked, "Do you have a baby?"

My chest tightened, vice-like and I couldn't speak. I shook my head 'no' as I reached for my tea.

"Tell us about your wife," said Madge, her eyes soft and sincere. "What does Lisa like to do?"

The tea wouldn't go down. I coughed and Gerald stood up preparing to hit my back.

Madge disregarded the coughing. I noticed that Madge was speaking in the present tense as if she knew how much I wanted to talk about Lisa. Even good friends had stopped mentioning her name, like she'd never existed.

"She's a dancer," I said finally. "Ballet."

"Lovely," said Madge. "I always wished for a daughter who would be a ballerina." She swept the boys with her eyes as if challenging them to find her one.

"That's Lisa's passion," I said. "She's elegant and graceful …and beautiful. She used to teach ballet in a studio off South Boulevard until enrollment dropped and we had to close it. Now she dances various parts for the civic ballet and sometimes travels out-of-town to dance a lead role or two."

"We're going to The Nutcracker," said Jake. "I have to go. My mom's making me."

"Lisa used to dance in The Nutcracker." My fork fell, clattering on my plate. "Sorry." I grabbed it. "Anyway, this year she didn't get a part." I didn't tell them how hard she'd worked to get back in shape for tryouts, how she'd refused to eat, what a tough time it had been…that life had become an express train with no opportunity to get off.

Everyone was looking at me, waiting. "She went to Tulane, actually started out in medical school, but it didn't take her long to discover that she was a dancer." I smiled, and added, "She's always in a hurry; always running, usually on her toes. I remember one of her friends asked, 'Why are you always running?' and she said, 'The faster I get there, the longer I can stay.'"

Madge and B.G. smiled politely.

"And she's always making do with broken things, and worn-out things because she won't take the time to get them fixed or get a new one." I laughed nervously, wishing I could shut up. "Like her handbag, for instance."

"Her handbag?" B.G. acted as if he were genuinely interested in my meager attempts at conversation. He helped himself to another load of rice and passed it to me.

I nodded. "This gray leather thing…"

From the green beans on her fork, Madge's eyes swept up at me.

Her look stopped me momentarily, then I finished, "…with a broken zipper."

She gaped. It became as clear to me as the realization in Madge's eyes: she had seen Lisa on the way to New Orleans. Confusion faded into light-headedness. Madge closed her mouth, but I had already panicked.

"I'd better be going," I said, pushing back my chair against stubborn carpeting. "I'm sorry to eat and run, but I have to get home."

"You didn't bring your car?" asked Eddie.

Robert tousled his hair as everyone laughed.

Standing, Madge said, "Everyone, please tell Mr. Despin goodnight."

"Thank you, Madge." I nodded, "B.G."

Madge walked me to the door. "The handbag!" she exclaimed in a whisper, eyes wide with astonishment. "Lee, on the bus, had a gray leather bag with a half ripped-out zipper!"

"I'll call you as soon as I sort it all out. I can't thank you enough." I started out the door, but paused when I overheard Eddie say, "He's like a Teddy bear, with hard clothes."

*　*　*

I went racing home only to lie in our bed and wait for dawn, groping for sleep that would not come to silence the spinning questions. *Could Lisa kidnap a baby? What if she did? What if she and the baby had both been kidnapped? Had she pretended that things were normal to keep from being killed?* Finally, I got up and made myself a cup of coffee to clear my head. It was the right thing to do, I decided, and phoned officer Blackburn to report my suspicions.

"There's a possibility," I said, "that my wife and the baby that disappeared at the same time are together." I couldn't bring myself to say what I feared.

"I appreciate your call, Mr. Despin, but it's our job to consider all the possibilities and I assure you it was one of the first things that came to mind. We've been working on the possibility she kidnapped that baby from the beginnin g."

He said it. I didn't have to. All along, that's what they were thinking. A sense of dread stole my breath, as I prepared to tell him about Madge Blalock.

"Everyone is a suspect, but no one is presumed guilty. It's an open investigation and anything could happen. You need to prepare yourself for that."

I hesitated. "Where are you looking now?"

"Everywhere. Hey look, Mr. Despin, if you know something…"

"I—I just thought of it."

"I'm with somebody right now." Blackburn's gruff voice was cautious. "How long'll you be there?"

"Well…"

"What say I drop by your office? Be there in an hour."

"Sure," I said, preferring the delay. "That's fine."

I hung up the phone and opened the refrigerator. Little remained of what Lisa had bought. Just condiments and some old celery that I'd soon have to throw out. I closed the door. Not much appetite. I walked down the hall to the baby's room and leaned on the doorframe, looking at the piled-up boxes of gifts never returned. Something had to be done about them. Lisa couldn't do it. Now I would have to decide, especially about the crib and baby chest.

* * *

Through the window, I saw that it was raining. I wondered if my folks had gone to the beach. Who had prevailed, my mother or my sister, Nan?

As usual when Mother had called, she asked how I was doing. "Fine," I lied. It was a game: meaningless question, meaningless answer.

"Your Dad and I are going down to the beach," she said, "and we were hoping you'd come along and get your mind off things."

"I can't, Mother... There's too much to do."

"Holden Beach is exquisite this time of year. I wouldn't miss it for anything. We've rented a house with a fireplace and two extra bedrooms. Billy and Nan are coming too. I told them we wouldn't go if it rains, but Nan's bringing her knitting and says she wants to go especially if it's raining. She wants to sit by the fire and work on another baby blanket. She's already on her second, and she's only four months along."

I almost said it was too soon to be doing that, but I caught myself and didn't say anything.

"Oh, Frank, don't worry about Nan. Nothing's going to happen. She's so..."

"So what?"

"So healthy. All my daughters have had healthy babies. You know that."

She didn't mean to say things that hurt, but there was so little to say that didn't hurt.

"I've really gotta go. It's time for work."

"Okay, but Frank, can I tell Nan what you've decided about handing down the crib and chest?"

I didn't know how I would do it, but I said, "Tell her I'll ship it."

* * *

Now, as I considered how hard it would be to actually go through with the promise, the phone rang. I jumped, then rushed to the kitchen and jerked it up, hoping.

"Frank? This is Madge Blalock."

"Madge. Hello."

"It may be none of my business, but I'd like to help."

I was silent for a moment, unsure of her intentions, unsure of my own. "Do you know about the missing baby?"

"I do now."

"Have you called the police?" My breathing stopped, waiting for her answer.

"Not yet."

I took a quick breath. "I did, just now. Blackburn said they'd been working on the possibility she'd stolen the baby since the beginning." I stalled. "I'm going to New Orleans and see if I can find her. Could you give me some lead time before you call?"

"All night I've been thinking. A woman out there is desperately missing her baby."

"I know."

"But Frank, you don't know. I kept imagining my daughter without little Maggie, the joy suddenly ripped from her arms, the hurting, the torment. Only a woman can understand that."

"Dammit!" I shouted, hitting the kitchen wall. "I do know! Four months ago, we had a baby, Lisa and me. She wasn't just a baby; she had a name. And she looked so healthy and cried so loud. You couldn't see anything wrong. Nothing at all. How were we supposed to know she had a heart defect? Something so rare it happens only once in 100,000 births? They didn't even know, till she died.

"Oh Frank…"

"When she was four weeks old."

"I should have…"

"How do you prevent something when no one knows what causes it?"

"I'm so sorry."

"And why do women think they're the only ones who feel? That's a bunch of crap!" My legs trembled, near buckling. "The father's supposed to hold things together," I told Madge, "stay in control. The father goes to the hospital to pick up the baby's things. He signs the autopsy report, makes the funeral arrangements. A mother can fall apart and the doctor gives her Valium to get through the funeral. The father gets his act together and goes back to work to pay the useless bill. What am I, some robot? Am I supposed to just keep on going, like nothing ever happened? Like we never had a baby? Like she never existed?"

Madge was silent.

"I'm sorry," I said finally," I didn't mean to shout."

"How can I help, Frank?"

"Just wait to call the police, that's all."

"Let me give you my daughter's phone number. Do you have a pencil? I'll call her so she'll be expecting to hear from you."

"You have your own family to worry about," I said, but I was thinking of mine. They'd been hard on Lisa, blaming her endless dieting and her rigorous performance schedule. And I'd never had the guts to defend her. I felt comfortable in their camp, being strong, because at least they weren't blaming me. I never said *it wasn't Lisa's fault; nobody's to blame*, and I had to wonder, *did I ever say it to Lisa?*

* * *

I took the ten o'clock flight out of Charlotte Douglas Airport and arrived at the Hotel Monteleon in New Orleans before eleven their time. I regretted leaving Madge wondering what happened to me, but I hadn't had time to think it over until I got on the plane. I just did what I had to do. She'd said she had to call the police, and though I understood, I also knew that I had to try to find Lisa first.

I slipped my key card into the door several times before the light flashed and I was able to turn the handle and get into my room. I tossed my carry-all with its two changes of clothes on the bed and opened the bedside table looking for the phone book. There was a name in the back of my mind of a friend that Lisa had known in college. I flipped to C and put my finger at the top of the column. Slowly I came down pronouncing the names. On the plane I'd been through the Ca-Co-Clu-Chi-routine mentally to no avail. It would come to me, I thought, when I saw it in writing.

On the third page, Cra…Craven. That was it. Now, which one? Probably near Tulane, but then I don't know the streets. I reached for my map. He was a professor. Biology, something scientific that she didn't like. Not biology, then.

I walked to the bathroom and took out my toothbrush. That's it. Anatomy. Gross Anatomy with the accent on gross.

I flipped to the back pages. Tulane Medical School. I dialed the number.

"Hello, I'm looking for a Doctor Craven, an anatomy professor. Is there someone by that name on your staff?"

"Yes, but he's out for lunch. May I take a message?"

"When do you expect him?"

"He has class at one, but he usually checks his messages when labs are over at six."

"Thanks," I said and hung up. I'd have to go catch him

before he went to class.

* * *

I was annoyed by the laughter in the slow elevator. The door opened onto a crowded lobby, clots of tourists stopping the flow. Finally, I hailed a taxi on Royal Street in front of the hotel as St. Mary's Cathedral chimed noon.

Out St. Charles Street, the taxi stopped in front of Charity Hospital. From there, I found the Tulane School of Medicine Building, its core swarming with men and women in brown coats. When I asked a secretary for Dr. Craven's office, she pointed toward a tall man with an armload of papers.

He looked up. "May I help you?"

"Frank Despin," I said, holding out my hand.

"Andy Craven." He shook my hand formally, then a flash of recognition. "Sure…" He shook my hand vigorously, smiling. "You're Lisa's husband. What brings you to New Orleans?"

"I'm looking for her, actually. I was hoping you'd seen her."

"Here?" I detected genuine surprise. "I haven't seen Lisa in…three years?"

"She's disappeared and I have reason to believe she came here."

"Disappeared? How do you mean that?"

"She just disappeared. I mean missing person, all that."

Andy shrouded his face with long, spreading fingers. "Why do you think she's here?"

"A tip," I said, pulling a snapshot from my pocket with a sweaty hand. "This was labor day weekend."

Andy studied the snapshot then handed it to the secretary who had stood up to look around his high shoulder, and held out her hand for it.

She took it in then arced her glance to Andy's face. "It's the woman I told you about," she said, as if pronouncing herself right. "It's the one with the baby, remember?"

"You thought she was lost?" Andy's eyes widened.

"This is the same lady. She was lost, all right." She shook her head as she plopped back into her chair.

Andy perused my face, for a long time, and perhaps a little suspiciously. Then he handed the stack of papers to the secretary and said, "Could you take these exams to my classroom and pass them out?"

"Sure. Should I stay?"

"Yes. I'll be there in a few minutes." He turned to me and motioned down the hall.

"Oh." The secretary stopped, and spun around on the ball of her foot. "Check your messages. One's from a police lieutenant."

"Thanks," he said, stiffening, but still walking. In his office, he nodded for me to sit. "What happened? Did you split up?"

"No, it's not like that," I said, wanting to be as quick as possible. "We lost a baby in June and she's had a tough time."

Andy kept his eyes on me as he slipped behind his desk toward the window.

"Not long after it happened," I added, "she had a big audition and failed to get a part, any part, even a small one."

Andy raised the blinds slowly, letting light flood the metallic space.

"She was wasted," I said, in words like a squeak. "So was I, but I couldn't..." My throat tightened and I couldn't swallow. "I was trying to be strong, and just keep going, and let her know I loved her anyway. She may have misunderstood."

Andy tipped his head back slightly to one side, moving one ear closer, like he heard exactly what I meant and agreed. He nodded sideways and pursed his lips into a pensive frown. He propped an elbow on his crossed leg and took his chin in hand.

"A few weeks later," I continued, "she disappeared from the dance studio, without her car... with nothing, like she'd been kidnapped. The police are looking all over, but not just for Lisa. They think she's kidnapped a baby."

His brow fell, his hand slipped up over his eyes. "And you think she came to me." He studied the floor, his shoes, mine, all the time shaking his head. "Why?"

"Because she came to New Orleans and you're here." This was the hard part; I'd always resented their friendship. I gripped my chair and swallowed. "She said you weren't lovers, but it doesn't matter now. If she's here, I just want to talk to her."

He pulled his chair closer to mine and leaned toward me. "She's right. We weren't lovers." He shrugged it off with a shoulder. "I would have liked it that way, but she was in love with you."

My heart rose and fell.

"Passionately," he said. "There's no one more attractive than a woman who's passionately in love. And it was you, the handsome man from a loving family who would give her every-thing she wanted in life...a rock to stand on."

He knew her well, I thought, glancing away. Lisa's parents had withdrawn support when she quit medical school to pursue a ca-reer in dance. They called her vain and irresponsible.

"So," he said carefully, "you know about the abortion."

Blinking, I tried again to look at him. "What abortion?"

"I thought she'd tell you eventually..." He leaned his face into both hands now. "After you married."

"She didn't." I recognized this as something I neither wanted to know or not to know. My heart grew brittle, like glass.

"I was new here," he said, "and still a sucker for a pretty girl's tears. Lisa cried through a whole class one day, and when it was over, I pulled her aside. I took her to my office to *do something*, I don't know, like give her a special assignment. She was failing the course. We agreed on a contract to get her grade up to a D and I felt like *The Hero*, until I found out she wasn't crying about failing my class. She was crying about an abortion."

"Your baby?" I asked with steely dread.

He looked up sadly. "Yours. Mardi Gras? 1975?"

The glass shattered. "Why?"

"Sleeping Beauty was never cast as a pregnant woman."

My posture, I noticed, was just like his, now. I sat up straight. "Why didn't she tell me?"

"Your family, your values."

"Damn my family!"

Andy lifted a hand to quiet me. "She said if you found out, you'd be ashamed of her."

"She told you!"

"At a weak moment. She regretted it. But, it was the beginning of a good friendship, and I'm thankful for that. Still, if she's here now, I haven't seen her."

"I'm sorry," I said, getting up like an old man. "Your class…"

He stood. "I'm sorry. If I see her…"

I gave him the hotel number and left.

* * *

There was no time to waste. If she weren't here, I'd try the Theatre of the Performing Arts. *What if the police already have her?* I all but ran. Down the hall, down flights of stairs, down another hall toward the entrance, past a student lounge. In the lounge, something caught my eye and I stopped. A gray leather purse lay on the coffee table, and beside it, a diaper bag.

My heart thundered. I turned to the small room, but how slowly my feet crept.

Lisa studied the selections in a coke machine. The fuzzy head of a baby bobbed over her shoulder. She turned toward me, reaching for her handbag.

"Lisa."

Blankly, she smiled. "No, I'm Lee," she said, fumbling with the zipper of her purse. "You must be..." When she lifted her gaze fully to mine, her eyes widened. What was there? Something less than recognition, but more than dismissal.

"Frank," I said, reassuringly, reaching for the purse.

She jerked it, protectively, to her chest.

"I'm Frank," I reassured.

"Hi," she said. She waited, suspiciously, as if to see what I would do.

What would I do? I stepped backward and drew a deep breath, trying to relax my chest. What do I say first? "I know how to fix it, remember?"

"Fix what?" She shifted the baby, but her eyes remained steady, on me.

"The zipper, remember? I can always get it."

Her stare cut through my soul. In her eyes, though, something powerful was dissolving. Slowly, I reached out; and this time, she let me take the purse from her hands.

Her mouth fell open and she staggered backwards into the coke machine, her face crumpling in recognition. She closed her eyes as if dropping a sheet over things intolerable, and the baby wailed.

Shocking Ernest Hemingway

Robert Wallace

Dearest Lori,
    I've been here almost two months now, but it seems longer. As for the hospital, it is no different from so many others I've seen: clusters of white-coated people walk the corridors, sick people come and go from rooms, food smells linger in the air, along with alcohol and disinfectant.

For two days now it has snowed. Not hard or anything. Just steady. Something in the order of six inches covers the ground. How odd to not see the grass. And it is nearly April! I bet you're just now seeing the first leaves on the oak trees. I miss their bright green. It reminds me of fresh mint, or better yet, lime sherbet. Some of the doctors continue to make fun of my accent, but it's all in good fun. I wonder, though, if they don't picture North Carolina as if it's in another country.

I miss you terribly. I have, as of yet, seen nothing of Rochester, though I am told there isn't much to see. The hospital has been gracious enough to give me a room until I can find something of my own. I look forward to finding a little apartment somewhere. Even though I've only been here a little under two months, living in a hospital makes me feel as though I'm at work all of the time. It's hard to let go of the things I see every day.

Darling, I still don't know about Easter. I'll let you know whether I can get off as soon as they tell me something. I so much want to go to Sunday service with you, feel your arm holding mine as we walk down the aisle. Have you purchased a new dress? I hope it's low cut. I like those best.

Love always,
Hayden

*　*　*

Mayo Clinic
April 2, 1967

Dear Lori,

Still snowing. It's so white outside, it's like God laid us a sheet over everything. The flakes have actually increased in size. I think if I held my hand out a window and there was a way to keep the snow from melting upon my open palm, that my hand would be covered in less than a minute. But perhaps I exaggerate.

I must go. Rounds in five minutes.

Hayden

*　*　*

Mayo Clinic
April 6, 1967

Dear Lori,

One birthday, when I was a boy, my uncle Burton gave me an electrical kit of sorts. He had made the contraption from an old tractor battery. Two wires, each about thirty inches in length, protruded from the battery, and attached to the ends of the wires were electrodes (nothing more than metal clips, really). Uncle Burton kept the battery charged only about half strength so that, at best, only a mild shock could be administered.

Boys can be given to moments of sadism, all in good fun, of course. My friend Duncan and I used to apply the wires to cats and dogs, mostly our own. What else were we going to do with it? I don't think it really hurt them.

Sometimes, if we wanted to, we could improve the shock delivery by securing a piece of metal to the animal. I'll never forget the day Duncan attached the electrodes directly to a piece of foil wrapped around a small poodle. He received some of the stimulus effect. That first time, Uncle Burton happened to be watching, and he laughed when Duncan jumped backwards, dropping the wires. He told us that wearing rubber gloves would protect us from the current.

Lori, that's why I'm here at the Mayo Clinic. I believe in electro-shock treatment, believe in its ability to alter a person's brain. Though the methods and instruments were rudimentary, shock treatment has been used since the 1930's, when the Hungarian physician Dr. Ladislas Maduna discovered that the brains of patients with dementia praecox had markedly fewer neuroglia than the brains of patients with epilepsy. He speculated that a voluntarily induced seizure would restore the normal balance of neuroglia cells. This initial seizure was induced in a psychotic mute man in his early thirties with an intramuscular injection of camphor-in-oil. Later, he utilized the compound Metrazol, which had been used as a safe way to induce seizures in livestock. It wasn't until 1938, at the University Hospital in Rome, that a seizure was first induced electrically.

These early crude delivery systems have gradually been replaced with more efficient ones. And protective measures have been instituted to decrease the likelihood of injury. It is my opinion that the treatment is safe and effective. Though, of course, not foolproof. But what is? Not even love is immune to an occasional shock. I cringe at the critics who don't understand. Some of them correlate lobotomy to electro-shock treatment. An absurd comparison in my judgment. But enough history, the rumor is that an important person is coming to the clinic for care. It excites me to know I can be a part of someone's resurrection.

I'm sorry I couldn't make it back for Easter. The snow only stopped yesterday. The airport resumed a full schedule of flights today. Frankly dear, I don't think I would have been able to get away. I just haven't been here long enough. I actually phoned, but when I heard your mother's voice, I hung up like a frightened schoolboy. Now tell me, why would I be afraid of your mother? Please don't tell her. Like you, she is vulnerable in my eyes. As for a wedding date, what do you think of the month of August? Let me know.

Love,
Hayden

*   *   *

Mayo Clinic
April 16, 1967

Lori,

You must promise to keep this absolutely quiet. The writer Ernest Hemingway arrived on the sixth floor two days ago. He came in with his wife and an entourage of friends.

Mr. Hemingway looked tired as he walked to his room the first time. He had a look of resignation about him. I've seen that look countless times already. He presents as a rather frail looking man, shorter than I would have thought, and a good deal lighter than he appears in pictures. His eyes are of the deepest brown with a speck of green. In their intensity, they remind me of cat eyes. Rarely do they blink, so I suspect he is paying attention to what is around him. He has a great thick white beard and a habit of looking over his shoulder. I have not been made privy to Mr. Hemingway's particulars, but I am told he will be administered electrotherapy. Dr. Leeland, the head doctor, will do the honors. I don't know yet whether I will be able to take part. I, of course, have pleaded to be allowed to participate.

So far, Mr. Hemingway has stayed mainly in his room. He's done no writing, that I know of. When I walk by his room, which has double-locked doors, I see him sitting up in his bed; his neck bent over a book. I don't know what he reads. I don't know if he talks to anyone. I see him sometimes walking up the hall, his head bent as if in thought. They have an orderly assigned to him, and they don't let him walk far. He's searched whenever he re-enters his room.

A new resident doctor arrived today. He's an odd fellow with cold, jumpy eyes. Already I have noticed he has marks on one of his wrists. He quickly pulled his lab coat down when he thought I was looking. He grinned at me, made me look away. His name is Randall. I don't want to accuse him of taking drugs but that's what I think he does.

Hayden

*　*　*

Mayo Clinic
April 24, 1967

Dear Lori,

I was telling Randall that you've read everything by Ernest Hemingway.

"I doubt it," he said. "Most women don't like Hemingway."

"Why?" I asked.

"He can be a bit raw, you know."

"Raw?"

"Must I spell it out to you, Hayden?"

So today I asked Mr. Hemingway for a copy of something.

I'm not sure why I thought he would have anything with him. And of course he didn't.

"I don't carry my books with me as though they were appendages, like my arm or foot," Mr. Hemingway said.

Can you send me something?
Yours always,

Hayden

P.S. I'm growing a beard. I hope you like it.

*   *   *

Mayo Clinic

May 9, 1967

Dearest Lori,

The concept of electrotherapy is to shock the brain into a convulsive seizure, thereby stimulating a chemical reaction that will improve mental functioning. Or rather, correct mental dysfunction. Several treatments are usually needed to arrest entrenched problems of thinking or acute depression. Often times, outpatient treatment is still necessary. The procedure is simple, really, though each step in the process is vital to ensure the desired outcome and prevent unwanted side effects or injury.

The patient is placed on his back on the treatment table. A sedative and a muscle relaxant are given simultaneously. Oxygen is delivered without interruption because the muscle relaxant prevents the breathing muscles from functioning. A paste is applied to the patient's skin and electrodes are attached directly to the temples. A patient's vital signs are monitored at all times, and they generally aren't aware that a seizure has been induced. The stimulus itself is administered no more than sixty seconds, if that long. The seizure can last twice as long, though the actual length is unknown. A piece of rubber is inserted in the patient's mouth to discourage injury to the tongue or lips.

Mr. Hemingway received his fifth treatment this morning. I've been present during the last three. He is a strong man, so his ankles and wrists require extra security. I held his face, this last time, even massaged his scalp a moment to relax the muscles. His hair is quite thin. His pants, which he insists on wearing, are loosened.

"Just relax, Mr. Hemingway," I told him.

He is quite compliant.

The anesthetist applied the oxygen mask, and I stepped aside. I am an observer here. Dr. Leeland applied the conducting jell, another doctor administered a muscle relaxant and a sedative intravenously. Electrodes were placed on Mr. Hemingway's sinuses and the seizure was induced.

Sometimes patients move; sometimes they don't. Theoretically, there should be little movement because of the sedation. I wouldn't say Mr. Hemingway bolted, but his midriff did come off the table. Standing behind him, I could have put my hand between him and the table. I seem to remember I might have, though I am not sure. I've never seen this happen before, not even when Duncan and I practiced on squirrels and rats. I noticed a flicker of alarm on Dr. Leeland's brow, though he was silent. Fearful that he might fracture his spine, I moved to apply pressure to Mr. Hemingway's belly, but Dr. Leeland startled me with his response. "No," he said, in a very firm voice. I took my fingers away as if they had touched an eye on the stove. Mr. Hemingway quieted soon enough and he didn't seem any more groggy than usual upon waking from sedation. An orderly escorted him to his room where he slept for several hours.

What I remember, in that brief moment, was the tautness of Mr. Hemingway's stomach: stretched like an overly inflated balloon. In the brief moment, too, came a tingle, not an energy discharge, but the grumbling of his own hunger.

Hayden

*   *   *

Mayo Clinic

May 11, 1967

Dear Lori,

Today I spent some time with him. He doesn't seem anything like you say he comes across in his books. He seems weary to me. Tired and vulnerable. Innocent. I know how he feels. This place can get you down. I've detected a melancholia in my own self lately.

We walked around the hospital, keeping on the well-swept sidewalk. It has been unusually warm here, though it is nothing like what it is in Raleigh. Along the edge of the sidewalk, anthills pop-up like miniature volcanoes.

While walking, he said: "I miss Cuba."

"What do you miss about it?" I asked.

"I miss my house, my books. I misjudged him," he said.

"Who?"

"Him."

"You mean Castro?"

"Yes. Castro," he said. "Bastard."

A Farewell To Arms remains on my nightstand, unopened. I think I'll leave it that way. I don't want reading it to influence my thinking of him one way or another. Randall says I'm just a prude. I tell him I think it's a matter of professionalism. He wonders if we aren't killing his spirit. I don't know what he means. Anyway, I'm sending the book back to you.

My dearest fiancée,

Love,

Hayden

*   *   *

Mayo Clinic
May 19, 1967

Dearest Lori,

Mary, Mr. Hemingway's wife, was able to spend the night with him, as a celebration of some sort. I don't know what they were celebrating, perhaps their anniversary. She has been staying at a nearby hotel and coming over twice daily. She looks tired, but talks about her husband's improvement. That night she slept over she brought with her a couple bottles of beer. They shared a drop or two with some of the off-duty staff. Unfortunately, it was my night to be on and I stood back from a distance and watched the proceedings. Dr. Leeland brought in his wife and children early on, and this seemed to me a bit much for him, though he remarked about the boy's curly locks.

Later in the evening, after her husband had been left to his dreams, Mrs. Hemingway confided in me that he had been talking about the Johnson administration, how his phone was certainly wiretapped. She has a beautiful face, Mrs. Hemingway, but sad eyes and the most beautiful red hair, or is it orange-red? Certain details like that escape me lately. It looked positively edible. She obviously loves him very much, and I couldn't help but wonder if we would have the same devotion to each other in our later years. She thought Mr. Hemingway needed to get off the ward some. I told her that I would mention this to Dr. Leeland. She thanked me and returned to his room.

Overall it was a quiet night. Little shouting. I did have to order a tranquilizer for one patient who got up in the middle of the night and pounded his fists on the nurse's station. I took him back without incident.

Hayden

    Racing Home

*　*　*

Mayo Clinic

June 4, 1967

Dear Lori,

In your previous letter you responded with displeasure, no, disappointment, in my refusal to read *A Farewell To Arms*. Perhaps if I was treating Mr. Hemingway's psyche through the use of psychoanalysis, reading any number of his books would prove beneficial. However, since I am not only insufficiently trained in the practice of psychoanalysis, and since that mode of treatment is scarcely used at the Mayo, any knowledge of Mr. Hemingway's writings, it seems to me, would be a waste of time. As it is, I spend a great deal of energy pouring over charts and records, interviewing patient's families, whenever they're available. Just last night alone, I copied a patient's chart and took it to my room to thoroughly read for the fourth time. This is a serious breach of protocol, but I thought it worth the risk. So you see, my dedication is unbounded.

Nevertheless, as you have so aptly pointed out, Mr. Hemingway is not my patient. In fact, I have taken a liking to the man and rather look forward to the walks we have been taking, almost daily. He wears these funny looking britches that rise high up on his stomach. The belt loops are well below the top of the fabric. The pants don't fit him well. Yesterday he must have stopped to adjust them three or four times. He appears to be losing weight.

Anyway, I digress. Please send me something. Randall says *The Old Man and the Sea* might be more to my liking. I have just read this over and it sounds a bit sharp-tongued. Forgive me, if that is the case.

Love always,

Hayden

*   *   *

Mayo Clinic
June 8, 1967

Dearest Lori,

The book arrived today. As I feared, you felt reprimanded by my last letter. I'm not sure what you meant by, "It's the least I can do," but no matter, it's here and I look forward to reading it. Let's forget the matter.

Hayden

*   *   *

Mayo Clinic
June 13, 1967

Dear Lori,

I do appreciate your quick retraction. At least that's how I interpreted the second paragraph. Let me say right off: there is no need for an apology. I don't consider you a sensitive female (I'm reading between the lines). As I've said, let's forget the matter. I also have been sorry in my time for things said or done.

But what did you mean by this?

"Try thinking your way to what it must be like to sit and look at the stars using your cupped hands, one on top of the other, like a telescope. All those stars within those tiny circles. Or after having lived in the city, one moves to the prairie and discovers for the first time that the celestial skies are irrefutably visible in the dark. Sometimes imagination is everything. Sometimes imagination is nothing."

And this?

"Taken by itself, the incident in the park wasn't the incriminating factor, but Hayden, you must know you frightened me, pulling on me like that, trying to get my finger to accept what it won't. There have been times I wondered if you belonged to the physical world. At times you've acted as though your life has been an unavoidable accident. Or punishment… That would explain everything. You seem to enjoy suffering, watching others do the same. This incessant knowledge of electricity. And yet there is something frightfully innocent about you.

"Now the belief you're treating others. How many voices can a body accept? Make sense of? How many bugs does a spider need before the web collapses?

"Mama says I shouldn't continue to write you. I told her I'm nineteen and need to make up my own mind about what is appropriate. And I figure reading about Ernest Hemingway is something you've already done. Reading what he has written might actually trigger some insight.

"You're where you need to be, though not where you think you are. Whenever I drive down South Saunders Street, I can see part of the hospital up on the hill. I wonder if you can see out your window, spot me driving by. A moving speck on wheels.

"Hayden, perhaps in time things will seem more clear. I truly hope so."

You certainly have a flair for words. My declarative sentences look rather simple next to yours. Let me just say this: testing that cattle prod on you was a mistake. I had no idea it carried that much voltage. Did you know your dress billowed up in the back when you ran away, exposing your panties? In my mind's eye I still see them as off-white. I remember the thought of the slippery material in my hand as I raced to catch you.

Love Always,
Hayden

*   *   *

Mayo Clinic
June 28, 1967

Dear Lori,

In all the annals of electro-convulsive therapy, as I know it, and I admit to not know the entire history, I don't know if I've heard of any patient responding to an induced seizure quite like Mr. Hemingway. In today's session he came in with one eye closed, the medications already working on him. But at closer inspection, I realized he was squinting, and the fat part underneath the closed eye (I forget which one) twitched like a nervous finger. It seems he has developed a tic, perhaps as a response to the procedure, or in anticipation thereof. Later when I spoke with Dr. Leeland, he dismissed it. He put it off as mere anxiety.

"Isn't that the same thing?" I asked.

"No. Anxiety is anxiety," he said. "If he had left with a twitch I'd be concerned. But he didn't."

"He was under sedation," I countered.

"I don't see a problem," he said.

The therapy room is a small one. So small that two persons can't walk around the table side-by-side. Mr. Hemingway was brought in by Randall. He kept his hand on him, too tightly in my opinion. I felt the pinch as if it happened to me. I told Mr. Hemingway to relax, breath normally. He smiled and tried to say something. I shook my head. He kept his eyes fixed on the ceiling. I tried to see what he may be seeing up there. After a few seconds I thought I saw movement and wondered if Randall might have pasted something on the ceiling: a black and white mobile, or a tiny drawing. But then it flew away and I realized it was only a fly.

I strapped Mr. Hemingway down, making sure the straps were properly cinched.

"Is it too tight?" I asked.

"No," he said. His voice was a whisper.

Randall had moved to the machine with Dr. Leeland. I could not see the dials.

Now, a certain amount of involuntary body movement is to be expected. But once again Mr. Hemingway's body lifted off the table. This time I moved to secure him before Dr. Leeland could say anything. If I would have had a small pillow, I believe I could have shoved it under him, felt the undercurrents of the electrical energy.

Love,
Hayden

*   *   *

Mayo Clinic
July 1, 1967

Dear Lori,

I hesitate to tell you this but if we are to be married I figure our closets should be emptied. Mine anyway. Here goes. My daddy spent some time in an insane asylum. This was when I was a boy of eight, I think. He used to pace the floors at night, talking to himself. Sometimes I'd hear him scream incoherent words. It frightened me, those screams. I'd cower underneath the blankets of my bed, the sweat dripping off my hot skin if it was summer.

Mama said it was because of the war. She used to try and comfort him, get him to come back to bed. One night I watched them in the living room. My bedroom door was barely open, but I could see them. Mama had her arms wrapped around Daddy's bare back; her arms dangled in front of his thin chest as if he was a boy. Maybe she had snuck up on him? I don't know. But he turned and smacked her across the face with the back of his hand. I wanted to run to her but I was afraid. She lay sprawled on the floor like a dead animal. My daddy bent over, pleading for her to get up. His small chest heaved.

"I'm sorry," he said. "Wake up, Livvy."

He had knocked her unconscious. She came to in a mi nute. Her jaw was already swelling.

That was the only time my daddy ever hit her that I can re-call. For the longest time I couldn't escape the vision of my mother going down. My daddy wasn't a violent man but he heard things.

That was the first time I saw what wasn't there to be seen.

I visited him once in the hospital. There were brick buildings everywhere. It seemed like a small city to me then. I wondered how it looked from the sky with all the lights on. My mama was with me, of course. We were ushered into a sitting room and Daddy was brought in by two men. He kept his hands together in front of him, though they weren't tied together. He seemed to be having great difficulty seeing, as if his eyes were focusing inward. I understood later that they had him medicated. He pulled a rock from his pocket.

"I found this in the yard," he said.

One side was smoother than the other with curved lines and small holes.

"This is from the beach," he said. He turned the rock over. "See these bits of shells."

I nodded.

"Now how do you suppose it got all the way over to Raleigh?"

"How?"

"Maybe at some point this land used to be sea."

I still have that rock. Keep it as a talisman. The rough side looks like a baby's foot, the small heel protruding at the bottom, no bigger than an adult man's pinkie-finger.

Hayden

*   *   *

Mayo Clinic
July 9, 1967

Dear Lori,

Did you ever want to run away, far away, and be someone else? Probably not. You seem sure about who you are. That's what

Mr. Hemingway said to me today as we took our walk. He pointed to a lone dove perching on a tree limb. He made aim, mimed shooting the bird. Above us the clouds and jet exhaust made a checkerboard design in the sky.

Randall was following us. I didn't care about his foolish giraffe-leg shadows stilting across the ground. I had a notion to turn around and expose him, but I figured that's what he'd want, just so he could deny it.

We walked along the path and on down to the picnic area. Below us some ducks bobbed for food in a small lake. Mr. Hemingway swiped his thinning hair to one side but it didn't move. He looked off in the distance, licked his chapped lips. What was he looking for? The words to his next book? Freedom?

I sat down with him at the picnic table. He had some conducting jell on his temples, and I wiped it clean with the tips of two fingers, then rubbed my hands together. He asked me if I thought he was getting any better.

"I can't be the judge of that," I said.

Then he said something peculiar. He said he wished he could be a wanderer, a gypsy, a traveler with a knapsack.

"I've not felt at ease in any one place," he said. "I've been racing home my whole life without ever knowing where home is." He paused. "How would you like to die?"

"A plane crash," I said.

"Just make sure you die," he said.

When we got back to the hospital, I was told Dr. Leeland wanted to see me. Randall was leaving Dr. Leeland's office when I walked in. I can still see his jumpy eyes bouncing in their sockets. For some reason the rest of him didn't look clear, like I was seeing him through greenish water. I had the feeling he had just informed Dr. Leeland something about me. You know, did you ever get that feeling? Some things you know without asking. Other things, you can't ask. And you never know.

Dr. Leeland was in his chair behind the desk. He brushed his waxy mustache.

"How is Mr. Hemingway?" he asked.

"He's. He's." I couldn't get it out.

"Depressed?"

"Yes. Depressed."

"He still talks to you?"

"Some." I reached for the rock in my pocket and rubbed the baby's heel.

"And the doctor? Is he still in there?"

I said nothing. Sometimes silence is best.

"I think your thoughts are still disturbing you. You may still be a problem for others. We'll need to up the shock dosage."

I didn't call him on the mistaken *you.* "I'll pass that on to Mr. Hemingway," I said.

Love,

Hayden

*   *   *

Mayo Clinic

July 31, 1967

Dear Lori,

I think about the old man in the skiff, fighting off the damn sharks. They circle the conquered marlin, their dorsal fins rising above the water. The oars aren't enough to keep them away. Sometimes they slap harmlessly against the sea. At other times the fish is hit, gouging a chunk of flesh loose. The oars splinter.

Do you remember going to the beach as a child? The water seemed to stop at some point in the horizon like a line on a piece of paper. Of course that was as far as the eye could see. The water goes way beyond that. And it makes waves out there, too. The sound absorbed into a fearless sky.

My daddy once said a drop of water from the middle of the

ocean takes fifty years to reach the shore. That drop of water is still out there, making its inevitable journey. It is older than me, older than time itself.

Mr. Hemingway will sign the book. I've drawn a picture of him on the inside of the back cover. His eyes look like mine. When I imagine the lilt of his pen, I think of you.

Love Forever,
Hayden

Stray

Cassandra Gainer

Hope was their second child, after Palmer, and they were at first assured that her condition was a fluke, a one in a million chance, the mistake of chemistry, nature gone awry. But with Kaitlin it was the same, though she looked flawless, with ten fingers and ten toes, curly hair, blue eyes that seemed to be dreamy with new life. It was then that the doctors told them it was the way their own loving bodies collided that caused this. Genetic. After Kaitlin's birth she and Richie did not make love for a year, some new fear grown between them, though it was something they never spoke of.

Now, each day was the same for Carly, a routine she could play backward, and forward, then backward again in her mind —first coffee with Richie, then cigarette, then Palmer up and ready for school, Richie to work, the school bus at 7:45, a little late some days, and then back inside to her girls. It was then that the real routine began, a careful test of memory on which so much depended—two milligrams of anti-seizure medicine for Hope, one for Kaitlin, 14 ounces each of blended baby food fed slowly from a syringe into the shunted holes in each of their stomachs, temperatures taken, baths on every other day, diaper changes, fresh clothes, then into the wheelchairs, Hope strapped down so she would not hurt herself, Kaitlin in leg braces to correct her growth. Some days there were doctor's appointments, physical therapy visits, emergency trips to the hospital, but most days it was just she and her daughters alone in the house and she would bake or sew or cook or clean the way her own mother had done, checking on the girls regularly as they twitched in their wheelchairs, silent.

She talked too, nearly constantly, the way a mother would talk to an infant, asking questions that required no answers, chiding and coaxing, but her daughters were no longer infants, they were three and five, growing girls. To Carly, the name of their condition was useless, an arbitrary language to which she had no real access, though through a litany of neurosurgeons, geneticists and specialists they had learned their daughters would get no better but no worse either. Neural Migration, they said. Neural Migration. The words felt angry in Carly's mouth, brutal syllables of consonants.

But things had gotten better eventually, though not easier. It was just that they were used to it and they were hopeful for their son's future, and could not imagine life without their daughters either. On her best days Carly felt as though she had been chosen and she remembered what a minister had told her once — God does not hand us that which we cannot handle. But sometimes Carly was angry. She would shout — at God, at her daughters, at women on the television screen who shamelessly plugged diapers, baby aspirin, paper towels, surrounded by their perfect children and husbands and homes, smug grins on their faces. It was when she shouted at her daughters that she felt the worst, though she could not help it. Sometimes she felt that Hope kicked her on purpose as she changed her diaper, or that Kaitlin cried too much and too long; she felt at times as if her daughters were withholding something, tricking her.

"Talk to me!" Carly would scream, her face hot and wet, her breath hissing through clenched teeth. "Talk to me for just once!"

Afterward she felt helpless and ashamed and she would lay her daughters on the floor and then lie down beside them and she would touch their hands and close her eyes and try to feel what they were feeling; sometimes she came very close, she thought, and she believed that there were two very real people inside of her daughters' seemingly uninhabited bodies. This is what haunted her. What if they were trapped somehow, trying to reach her, and it was only that she could not understand? Some nights in bed she listened for hours to Richie breathe, his hand on her stomach or thigh, and she thought about all the languages she could not speak, and Morse code, and the high, inaudible whistles that only dogs and fish could hear.

*　*　*

This year, Palmer had decided, he would be Dracula for Halloween because it was a scary costume, and also a little funny too, like Count Chocula on the box of cereal he ate for breakfast each morning. Carly and her son planned his costume—white makeup, a black cape, slicked hair and, of course, the teeth and real blood.

"Well, not real blood," Palmer said. "But, you know, the fake blood that looks real."

Carly agreed to the costume, and while he was at school she set out her sewing machine on a card table in the family room and began to sew the cape out of black nylon, and also started on costumes she had picked out for the girls. A brightly colored court-jester costume for Hope, and a gauzy, pink princess dress for Kaitlin. This year Palmer had decided he was too old to go trick-or-treating with his mother in tow, and instead, Richie would dress up and go with him, like one of the boys.

"Only babies go with their mother," Palmer said.

Carly decided she would stand in the front yard and give out candy to the children with Hope and Kaitlin so that they could watch Palmer as he went from door to door. She was proud that Palmer was not afraid to go without her this year, but also a little sad. Not so long ago he had clung to her. She remembered a time when, less than a week after Kaitlin's birth, Palmer had pleaded with her to accompany his kindergarten class on a trip to a local farm. It was early spring and in the barn they found a just-born calf, still trembling slightly against the stall. Palmer was fascinated and had reached to touch it. When Carly leaned down, the tiny creature had pressed its muzzle to her chest and its high-pitched yelps touched her in a familiar, aching place, causing milk from her swollen breasts to soak her T-shirt, leaving perfectly round, wet circles. She wore her sweater the rest of the day, but she was secretly elated at her body's mysterious yearning, its primitive response that was beyond her control. Soon after, with Kaitlin unable to nurse, Carly's milk dried up and every momentary thought of the calf was like a cruel reminder of what she would never experience again. Even now, the memory was like a new, pink scar.

At three o'clock, Palmer came home and found her angry, ripping out a seam of Kaitlin's costume again and again, trying to get it straight. He looked at her quizzically then went to the kitchen for a soda.

"A kid on my bus got bitten by a stray dog," Palmer said, standing in the kitchen doorway. "They can't catch the dog so now the kid might have babies."

"Babies," Carly said, glancing absentmindedly at the girls. "I think you mean rabies, Palmer."

"Oh," he said.

*　*　*

Darkness was just setting in, and only a thin line of light sky striped the horizon. Parents passed carrying their youngest children, tired from the night's excitement, and the older kids began to flood the streets in store-bought masks and homemade getups, some wearing only the faintest suggestions of costumes—a hat, a mustache—as if to prove they had outgrown the holiday but still wanted to cash in on the treats. Carly watched four girls totter toward her on high heels, their thin, still-girl legs wobbling with the unfamiliar height, off-balance. Their faces were done in carefully applied make-up—orangy base, the bluest eye shadow, black, black eyeliner, and dark red lipstick that bled from their lips onto their still unblemished skin. They wore mini-skirts and half-shirts and had streaked themselves with body paint. Carly noticed that one of the girls had not shaved her legs and she remembered with pleasure this small window of time between childhood and womanhood, at twelve or thirteen, when life still glimmered in the distant future like a heat mirage and everything was safe and new and possible.

"Trick or treat!" the girls shouted in unison.

"And who are we?" Carly asked.

One of the girls, the tallest and prettiest, clearly the leader, dropped her arms to her sides in exasperation.

"We're supposed to be the Spice Girls, duh, but never mind," the girl muttered, and turned to go, glancing for just a moment at Carly's daughters in their jester and princess costumes. She rolled her eyes again. Her ankle turned suddenly and she dropped to one knee, catching herself on the arm of Kaitlin's wheelchair. She pulled her hands back quickly as if she had touched hot steel.

"Whoa," she whispered under her breath, and stared for one more moment at Kaitlin before turning to go.

Carly watched the girls as they continued down the street, stopping at each house, their high, reedy voices piercing the night with giggles and girlish squeals. She felt suddenly angry and ashamed.

"You hate these costumes don't you," she asked fingering the soft felt of Hope's jester hat. "These aren't what you would have chosen at all."

She was tired, she realized, and she decided to take the girls inside and wait for Palmer and Richie to get home. She put the bowl of candy on the ground and then turned the girls' chairs around, one at a time, to face the house.

There were strange shadows mounting in the darkness, cast from the jack-o-lanterns that sat in a neat row on the porch. A big one cut by Richie, a medium one cut by Palmer from markings Richie had carved into the soft flesh of the pumpkin, and three small ones—one for Carly, one for Hope and one for Kaitlin—that Carly had cut into careful, smiling faces with sharp triangle eyes and noses that glowed from the inside out. In the distance Carly heard screams and she imagined Richie jumping from the bushes to scare groups of Palmer's friends from school as they passed. Palmer would double over in laughter and point the way he did when Richie tickled her or made rabbit ears over the girls. She felt a little better then, thinking of Palmer and his heavy sack of candy she would have to wrest from his fist as he slept later that night.

Out of the corner of her eye she saw her neighbor Tim motioning in frantic gestures from his porch, and she could hear him shouting her name again and again. She felt disoriented and confused for a moment but this quickly turned to fear as she realized Tim's children were running up the lawn to their porch. The hair on the back of her neck stood on end and she could feel the presence of danger unseen and unnamed, and she began to make out Tim's words slowly—watch out for serod, biglog, hotrod, the dog. The Dog.

It was then, as if naming it, saying the words made it real, Carly saw the creature, a wild, unkempt thing gathered onto its haunches as if preparing for attack, the pricks of its ears flattened, the starved ribcage heaving. Carly spread her arms and backed toward her daughters, and she could feel a thin bile of fear rising in her throat as she watched the stray dog circle them slowly; she gagged slightly at the tufts of hair rising from the matted, scabby back, the scarred hole where an eye should have been. She tried to think of what to do, what to say — lunge, scream, coax, wait — but it was too much, she could be neither brave nor smart at this moment; she could think of nothing. Behind her she could hear the friction of one of her daughters twisting in her chair, a seizure, and she flattened her body to the backs of the wheelchairs, trying her best to cover the movement and noise. Her daughter groaned wildly and tossed her head from side to side. The dog growled in response then circled to face Hope and Kaitlin and crouched on the ground, watching. Carly turned slowly too, trying not to startle the dog to any action. A minute passed and she could see at the edge of her vision Tim crouching in the bushes with a rifle pulled close to his body.

The dog got up with a start and circled, stopping again in front of the girls. Carly watched him carefully as he seemed to look from one girl to the other. She couldn't breathe as the dog drew closer and then, with a small shudder, sat and rested his head in Hope's lap. Hope's seizure had begun to subside and she was grunting softly, uhn, uhn, uhn, uhnuhnuhn, and the dog sighed and began to whine softly also. Minutes passed, Tim creeping closer each second, the dog resting in Hope's lap, his eye turned upward toward her pale, wild face, and Hope slowly lulling herself back to sleepy calmness. Kaitlin twitched slightly and began to coo and the dog lifted its head and gave one short bark. He backed up then, sniffing the air as if sensing danger, then nuzzled Kaitlin's hand once before turning quickly and loping off toward the open cornfields that surrounded the subdivision.

Carly couldn't move and she watched the graceful arc of his body propelling him toward safety until he stopped abruptly at the edge of her yard where it met the fields. He turned then slowly and seemed to be looking at her and she felt some cavity of her heart deepen and expand around the knowledge that some wish had come true before she had even known she wished it. It seems silly, she would say later, but he was looking at me. Then Tim fired a shot into the air and the dog was gone.

Neighbors rushed to her, surrounding her and her daughters as if to protect, but she was calm and unafraid as if in a dream and she wheeled her daughters into the house while Tim used her phone to call animal control.

"Could have damn near killed you all," Tim said. "I just couldn't get a clear shot."

"No, no, of course not," Carly said, shaking her head, and her own voice was foreign to her, ghostlike. She heard the door slam then as Richie and Palmer returned, rushing into the living room to find Hope and Kaitlin already asleep in their wheelchairs.

"Christ almighty, I heard what happened, is everyone all right here?" Richie asked. "Carly?"

It was then that Carly began to shake, her breath escaping in small bursts until Richie pulled her to him and held her hard against his body, and she began to sob.

"No, no, honey. It's all right, everybody's okay. It will all be okay, Carly, I promise," Richie said, his own breath coming unevenly.

"Oh Richie, it was all wrong," she said between sobs. "The costumes, I mean, they were so wrong, it's not what they wanted at all, I just didn't know."

"It's okay, we'll figure it out hon, it's all okay now, I promise, I'm here," he said.

"Yes, yes, I know," Carly said, but there was an ache in her chest she could not soothe. The dark image of the dog hovered at her mind's edge like a word that was just at the tip of her tongue, a question she could never remember to ask. Richie, she knew, could not help her figure it out.

She went then and got the girls ready for bed while Richie helped Palmer sort his candy. Changing her daughters out of their costumes and into clean pajamas and diapers, she heard Palmer counting methodically and then Richie interjecting random numbers, trying to confuse Palmer's count.

"Dad, you rat!" Palmer said, laughing, then began his count again.

"Fourteen, six, one hundred and seventy-one-one-one-one," Richie chanted.

"Dad!"

It was a game like the many others between them, father and son, and she smiled to herself as she settled the girls gently into bed, quilts tucked neatly around them, safety bars drawn up. She sat rocking in the same chair she had rocked them to sleep in as babies and, when she was sure they were asleep, she stood over them and watched their chests rise and fall in even, synchronized rhythms. Asleep they looked like any other little girls, their faces slack and calm, hands curled into small fists and tucked to their chests. Leaving their room, she picked up Hope's jester outfit and, drawing it to her face, breathed deeply. There was the faint cold-ammonia smell of fur and dirt, a feral scent that had faded to just a subtle trace that was barely detectable among the scents of baby powder and new fabric. Carly took the costumes to the garage and placed them at the bottom of the garbage pails under bags of kitchen trash and old newspapers.

That night in bed she thought she could hear a low and distant howl, a faint thread of rage or pain that wove its way into her sleep so that she dreamed of wolves throughout the night, their steel-gray fur bristling as they circled in a tight pack, their black eyes glistening to a deep gold. She woke with a start in the still-dark morning to the sound of one of her daughters moaning softly from her bedroom down the hall and she remembered suddenly the dog, the graceful slope and pull of its muscles in flight, the backward glance that would be remembered in her bones forever like a mended break. She rose and followed the steady hum of her daughter's voice down the hall and stood outside the open door. She could see out the window to the yard and to the fields beyond and the morning was gray and wet, and she thought of the dog darting through woods and across great expanses of deep green pastures, racing home over hills and hills and mountains and she thought suddenly of an old word her grandmother had used, Godspeed, Godspeed. Carly stood there for a very long time, and she was still and quiet, watching the morning lighten to a milky blue sky, listening to her daughter, uhn, uhn, uhn, uhn, uhnrunrunrunrunrunrunrun. Run, Carly thought. Run.

This Blood's for You

Christopher Farran

This could be the week after all, Ronnie was thinking. This could be the week his luck changed.

He passed old Gimpy Roberts going down the backstretch into turn three and pitched the car sideways on the orange clay. By the time he reached the starter's stand again he had half a lap on everybody.

Somewhere in the infield Sharon the Trophy Queen was watching him; watching him as he slid through turn one with only four laps to go; watching him as that $500 paycheck got closer. She was wearing that little yellow thong bikini, watching him as he accelerated down the backstretch and felt the motor shudder.

Watching him as he felt a POP somewhere and smelled bitter smoke and saw the tach take a dive.

Ronnie shoved in the clutch to save what was left of the motor and pulled into the infield and coasted toward his trailer. He knew the drill. This was his destiny, brother. Every damn week. He turned off the ignition and sat in the smelly car and pulled off his helmet. He wasn't thinking of Sharon the Trophy

Queen or the lost $500 or the blown head gasket or whatever the hell it was. He was wondering if he had enough gas in the truck to get him home.

*   *   *

It was time to reevaluate, soon as he had dinner. But why weren't the catfish biting?

The slippery creek bank was mossy and wet under his butt and he could hear the mosquitoes on the back of his neck. He kept the fishing line in the canal. It was past midnight and he could see the bats darting after their snacks in the still air over the water. He wondered where the copperheads were.

He had wanted to stop for a burger on the way home from the race track but he didn't have the money in his wallet. He had looked in the refrigerator in his trailer home and saw nothing but an open can of dog food, so he'd stepped outside with his fishing pole and caught him a cricket. He had fished along the canal many a time, but that was for relaxation; this was for dinner.

He knew what they called him at the race track. Every week he led the feature and then dropped out. 'Premature Evacuation' they called him for his weekly DNF. He jiggled the fishing pole and said out loud, "I tell you what, I'd sell my soul right now for a winnin' race car."

TzBAM! He jumped and yelled at the flash of light and the thunderclap. Next to him was a sulfurous cloud of yellow smoke. Stepping out of the cloud was a dark-haired clean-shaven man with a big toothy smile and a white linen suit.

And Ronnie knew him; had seen him on the TV after midnight many a time. As the cloud of smoke dispersed, the man stepped forward and held out his hand:

"L.T. Penry," he said. "Penry's Mattress Warehouse — Three Locations." His handshake was firm and confident.

Ronnie had invited a pact with the Devil. What he got was a

sponsor.

* * *

"Let's go have us a drink," L.T. said. "You got a lot to celebrate." He drove Ronnie in a white Cadillac to the U.S. 311 North Roadhouse where he proceeded to order one of everything, plenty of ice, thank you honey. The band was packing up and the place was near empty; Ronnie nursed a single Jax beer as Mr. Penry tossed down a margarita and ordered a shot of Southern Comfort. He polished off a Rusty Nail and asked the waitress for a Bloody Mary.

"Anything you *don't* drink?" she asked.

"Don't never bring me no frog's blood," L.T. said.

"It wouldn't of occurred to me," the waitress assured him.

"Dangerous stuff," L.T. winked at Ronnie and flashed his bicuspid smile. "I react to it."

* * *

Ronnie knew that somewhere down there in the infield Sharon the Trophy Queen was watching him as he thundered down the front stretch with the tach pegged at 7700 rpm. He knew she could see the new white lettering on the side of the car — Penry's Mattress Warehouse — Three Locations — and he knew she was waiting for the same thing he was: the sudden shudder, the pop, the acrid cloud of white steam, the silence as he coasted to a stop in the infield.

He had half a lap on old Gimpy Roberts with two laps to go. Down the backstretch he could see the old men in their bib overalls and the pimple-faced kids watching him with their mouths open, waiting for disaster to strike.

But he was laughing as he went under the checkered flag. No more premature evacuation. He had finally come all the way.

It wasn't just the $500, either. For years he'd stood in the

crowd at the edge of Victory Circle while other drivers—
younger guys—stood next to Sharon in her little yellow thong
bikini. Sharon and the winning driver faced the photographers
and the adolescent boys and Ronnie knew what was happening
on the dark side of the circle: the winning driver was rubbing his
greasy fingers across Sharon's bare butt, dimpled with goosebumps
while she smiled in the cool night air.

Now it was Ronnie's turn. As the flashbulbs sparked in his
eyes and the promoter stood to one side with a fake blowup of a
$500 check, he snuggled up next to Sharon and put his arm
around her back and rested his hand on her naked hip. When she
handed him the trophy he said, "Hey, get your clothes on and
let's go spend some of this money." He noticed a small bruise on
her lovely neck, almost like a hickey.

*   *   *

Ronnie was putting the race car on the trailer when L.T.
Penry told him he didn't have time to date. "I got you an appearance tomorrow morning at the Yadkin River Shopping Mall in
Stoneville," he said. "You just got time to take a shower, hose off
the race car, and drive on up there."

And Sharon the Trophy Queen told him, "Not tonight,
Ronnie. You got a nasty look in your eye, and your hair smells like
rotten eggs."

Ronnie went home and looked in the mirror. It was true
that his eyes had become a hard, flinty yellow; and it was true that
no matter how often he showered and brushed his teeth, his hair
and his breath still smelled like sulfur. He was afraid to tell Sharon
the rest: that when he put his hand over his heart for the playing
of the national anthem at the race track, he couldn't feel his
heartbeat; and it'd been weeks since he'd called home to say hey to
his mother.

*   *   *

It would have been a cakewalk Saturday night at Tri-County Speedway except for two things. The good news was that he drove like a demon and the car ran like a dream; he won the purse and an extra $100 for leading the most laps. The bad news was that the crowd was *booing* him in Victory Circle when Sharon handed him the trophy.

And Ronnie knew why: after qualifying that evening, old Gimpy Roberts and a young driver named Cody had come up to him in the infield and asked if they could borrow some spare parts and tools. Cody, who needed a special drill, wasn't a problem: he was a fast, handsome, cocky little sonofabitch and Ronnie figured he could damn well pay his own dues the way Ronnie had paid his. Ronnie said Sorry, he couldn't help.

Gimpy Roberts was a different story. He was probably 55 now, and way past his best years, but he had been track champion five times in the past and he was still a crafty old galoot. He needed an ignition coil and when Ronnie said no, he was aware that Gimpy was probably the most popular driver in three states.

On the half-mile dirt tracks, that kind of stuff gets around fast; and when Ronnie loaded his race car on the trailer after winning the race, a sheriff's deputy had to stand between him and the pissed-off race fans.

Ronnie heard a voice behind him telling the deputy, "Out of the way, boy; L.T. Penry—Penry's Mattress Warehouse— Three Locations."

Ronnie turned to Penry and said, "Let's get out of here; I need some sleep."

"You can sleep tomorrow night," Penry told him. "I've entered you in a big-money race tomorrow afternoon up at Granite Lake. I might open me a new Mattress Warehouse up there and we need the exposure."

"Granite *Lake*?" Ronnie said. "That's 200 miles!"

"You got a problem with that?" Penry said. "Ain't you forgettin' something? I *own* you, buster!"

* * *

A big-money race attracts racers from Ohio and Wisconsin to Missouri and Florida. Sure enough, they were all there—and Ronnie cleaned their clocks. One hundred laps, thirty starters, a track he'd never seen before—and he made 'em look silly. He got his picture in all the newspapers and went racing home exhausted, but with a check for ten thousand dollars in his pocket.

Which L.T. Penry relieved him of, late that night when he pulled into the driveway of his trailer home, and paid him his usual $500 salary. "You got to be at Southside Baptist Church for the 11 a.m. service tomorrow," Penry told him. "We got to work on our image."

Ronnie cleaned up and did as he was told; but he noticed that the old ladies in the church pew near him moved away because of the rotten-egg smell in his hair.

* * *

Tuesday, Ronnie stopped by the community college where Sharon was taking accounting, to have lunch with her in the cafeteria. He wanted to know—and sort of didn't want to know—where those bruises on her neck were coming from.

Sharon leaned across the veal cutlet on her tray and said quietly, "That sleazebag sponsor of yours keeps tryin' to bite my neck."

"*Penry!*" Ronnie said.

"He comes by the trailer park after midnight. Last weekend my little boy had to run him off with his baseball bat." Sharon said, "Rusty needs a new catcher's glove, too, but I don't know where the money's gonna come from."

Ronnie was fed up with the way L.T. treated Sharon and him, acting like they were his own personal property. After lunch he drove to the Mattress Warehouse on Sandy Ridge Road; but of course they told him that Penry was at another location, just like they always did.

On his way to the Mattress Warehouse at Union Creek, Ronnie realized he had never seen L.T. Penry during the daytime. The noisy SOB showed up only at night.

Saturday night after he'd won the feature at Delta Speedway —first race he ever won there in six years of trying—Ronnie found Penry in the winner's circle where Sharon was handing him the trophy and Penry was thanking her by trying to kiss her on the neck—with his teeth.

"Mr. Penry!" Ronnie said. "I'm givin' you a lot of good publicity with this car, but if you don't keep your mouth off'a her neck, you're gonna have to find you another driver."

Sharon looked embarrassed but Penry turned on him as soon as they were out of the light. "How'd you like a good hard wreck just to remind you where your good fortune comes from?" he hissed. "I can arrange it, you know."

*   *   *

Ronnie was depressed. Monday after dinner he called Sharon the Trophy Queen. "I'm makin' good money, I've paid off all my bills, but I can't put up with this," he told her. "What am I gonna do?"

He called her because his instinct told him he could trust her. She was divorced and a single mom, going to the community college by day and working nights at the hospital laundry. She longed to get out of that yellow thong bikini the way Ronnie longed to get out of his bargain with L.T. Penry.

It galled him that L.T. was sending him further and further away every weekend to race tracks and shopping malls while he was leaving those little hickey marks on Sharon's neck.

"You're givin' him what he wants," was her advice. "Give

him what he *don't* want."

Ronnie thought about that and asked if her little boy Rusty was there. "He's doin' his homework," Sharon said.

"Put him on," Ronnie said. He said to the boy, "Your momma says you need a new catcher's mitt."

"Yes sir," the boy said hoarsely.

Ronnie liked a boy that said Yes Sir. He said, "Tell you what, Rusty. You bring me four or five frogs—big ones—and I'll take you out to K-Mart to get you a new catcher's mitt."

There was a long pause. Rusty was wondering if he was selling his soul for a new Little League glove. Then the boy said, "Live ones?"

Next afternoon there was an old coffee can on Ronnie's front stoop with five big bullfrogs in it. He performed the messy operation in his bathroom shower stall so he could wash it out easier, filled an empty Budweiser bottle halfway up with the frogs' blood, and hammered a cap onto it.

It was Halloween night and Ronnie was eager to get out of the house before the neighborhood goblins showed up because he was too cheap to buy candy. He backed the race car out of the truck, fired it up, and drove off through the night to L.T. Penry's house.

*   *   *

Penry lived up on top of a hill in a big pretentious brick mansion with four white columns on the front veranda. Ronnie pulled up in the paved driveway and revved the car's 406 short-block until the motor howled and Penry had to come to the front door to see what the racket was.

"Hop in," Ronnie said. "I'm takin' you for a short ride so we can celebrate something special."

"I just got home," Penry pleaded. "I been…workin' late."

"Won't take but a minute," Ronnie said. "Sharon gave me an

idea. Who knows, you might wind up with *five* Mattress Warehouses."

Ronnie had said the magic words, and Penry squirmed into the race car on the right side. "Damned uncomfortable," he whined.

"Ain't it, though?" Ronnie said.

When Penry was settled in, Ronnie headed for the canal, keeping the RPMs up and the speed over 90, sliding the car's back end through the curves.

"Back off!" Penry said. "This thing ain't got no headlights!"

"Don't go complainin' to me," Ronnie said, "I ain't got no soul."

When they reached the canal, Ronnie hung a left and accelerated. The dirt path ran alongside the murky green water for a couple of miles, straight as an arrow under the willow and oak trees. He pushed the throttle down and gunned the car up to 125.

"Let me out," Penry ordered. "You forgettin' who you work for?"

"I'll let you out as soon as you drink this cocktail," Ronnie told him, and handed Penry the beer bottle. He punched the pedal and got the car up to 135.

"*What?*" Penry pushed the cap off the bottle and smelled the contents. The dark trees flashed by on either side of the car and the engine bellowed.

"This road ends at that old abandoned fish camp," Ronnie reminded him. "About two miles, and these brakes are gettin' mushy."

"We'll go into the lake," Penry wailed, "and I cain't swim!"

"You won't have to," Ronnie shouted. "The impact will kill us." He goosed the accelerator and the car was going close to 150 miles an hour. They were in a tunnel now, with the dark trees on either side and the moss and vines forming a black roof over their heads. Ronnie had never driven a race car this fast.

"Ronnie, we had us a *deal*," Penry shouted. "What is it you *want?*"

"I want you to drink up," Ronnie said. "Look up yonder."

Ahead of them in the distance the ruins of the old fish camp were silhouetted against the moonlit lake. The speedometer said 160 miles an hour.

Penry screamed, "NAAAaaah..." and raised the beer bottle to his lips.

TzBAM! There was a flash of light and a thunderclap and the inside of the car filled with a yellow cloud of sulfurous smoke. Blinded, Ronnie stood on the brakes and fought to control the car.

The race car fishtailed right and then left, bouncing and shaking and showering sparks and bits of sheet metal as it careened between the trees.

Ronnie pumped the brakes and sawed at the steering wheel. The wheels locked up, the hood flew off, and the car spun around backwards. Ronnie thought, "Oh Lord, they'll never find me out here!" The car plowed backwards into the rotten wood and collapsed debris of the old fish camp.

In the silence, Ronnie sat there and began to think that he'd lucked up. Then he looked down and saw his legs soaked with blood. He groaned and tried to move. When he touched his blue jeans and smelled his fingertips he recognized the stuff: the watery pink frogs' blood, stringy and slippery. The broken beer bottle was on the floor of the car. L.T. Penry was gone.

He climbed out carefully, leaving the shattered race car steaming and smoking where it was. In a moment, the crickets and cicadas and ditch frogs started up again, and Ronnie began to walk.

*   *   *

Sore and tired, it took Ronnie a couple of hours to walk the length of the path back toward the highway. It seemed like a long time ago that he and Penry had sat in the 311 North Roadhouse and Penry had drank everything in sight. Well, almost everything. Sharon's advice had reminded him of it.

By the time he reached the highway the canal on his left seemed darker and he could see the tops of the trees outlined against the lightening sky. He stood on the shoulder of the road and waited.

The first car that came along still had its headlights on.

Ronnie stuck out his thumb, embarrassed by the dried blood on his jeans. The car slowed down and he thought it looked familiar. It pulled over toward him and Sharon the Trophy Queen leaned over to open the right-side door.

"Ronnie!" she said, and she seemed glad to see him. "Bless my soul, are you all right?"

He looked carefully, but the bruise marks on her neck seemed to have healed completely.

She said, "Look here, I just dropped Rusty off at school. Come on home with me and I'll pull those dirty old jeans off of you and throw 'em in the washer."

Namesake

Anne C. Barnhill

Funny about names. You might guess that my great uncle Edwin was a lifelong bachelor with thin, narrow shoulders and close-set eyes that pinched together when he tallied his ledgers. And you'd be right, of course. That's exactly what an Edwin would look like.

Change but a few letters and you alter a man forever.

An *-ard* instead of the *-in* at the end of his moniker would have given my uncle a kingly name—Edward. Legs thick and steady at the bow of a ship, well-muscled arms guiding the wheel. Even the rough seas would not stir such a man and dark thunderclouds would find a permanent home in his eyes.

Rather than captain ships, Uncle Edwin built them. More specifically, he owned a company in Boston that manufactured vessels for the United States Navy during the War Between the States. It's unlikely that Uncle Edwin could have managed to nail one plank aboard the bow, but he knew how to run a profitable business and exact an honest day's work for little pay.

Yes, my uncle fit his nomenclature and died of consumption in mid-life, at the beginning of the last decade of the last century, the Nineteenth. How antiquated that sounds! Not modern like our new Twentieth, with its automobiles and electricity. Though I was born in the late 1800's, I welcome the promises held in the word "twentieth," a coming-of-age for the whole world. And to carry me into that fashionable time, I've a small share of Uncle Edward's money.

His nest egg, for so he always called it, was much larger than the phrase implies, and came to my father, Wallace, a greedy name which didn't fit the mild-mannered parent whose pale features I inherited.

My name is Edwina, after my uncle, who hoarded his money, neither marrying nor giving a dollar to nieces and nephews on holidays. At his death, his detailed instructions for an ostentatious funeral were carried out to the letter by my father, who seemed quite embarrassed by the entire event. A church full of flowers and not a soul there for the service, except, of course, our little family, Mother, Father, my brother, George, and myself.

Father, finding himself not a builder of any sort, sold the company and took Mother and me to Charleston, South Carolina, where the year-round warmth soothed his joints and Mother found solace in the large Episcopal Church where she sang alto in the choir. George was left in Boston, in a proper boarding school for boys his age. Mother explained such schooling was the custom among the rich and now that we could afford things, George would receive the very best. She made no mention of what I might expect.

Upon our arrival in the sun-filled South, I, Edwina, took to considering the sounds in a name, the power you call up when you declare a thing.

My own designation is a form of the masculine, but the added syllable gives it a shrill, irritating resonance. As a result, I feel as if the name is a kind of diminutive, though I know better. I certainly feel less than a man, not as important, or as interesting. I feel less even than a narrow man like Uncle Edwin. My hair, pulled away from my face to add a sense of fullness, is pale brown. Some call it mousy, but I prefer to say bunny brown. Rabbits are superior rodents, after all. And my eyes, by some genetic miracle the exact same shade as my hair, are too close together, shaped like small quail eggs.

Maybe not. Could be my hair is thick, raven-colored and my eyebrows spear their points into my forehead with brutal force. And my eyes. The deep, steely gray of bullets circled by a darker ring around the iris. A mouth, not whitish and drawn, but red and indefinite, a blood smear.

But no, you were right the first time. An Edwina couldn't be as dramatic as that. An Edwina would be a spinster and all that word implies. Nothing could grow on an Edwina, except thoughts, barbed jealousies of all the Clarissas and Juliannas that swirl across the ballroom floor while Edwina stands over the punch bowl and feigns fascination with sherbet.

An Edwina would be the butt of jokes from nasty little boys. Oh, the humiliation. The event recalled still turns my pasty face a mottled pink.

One Sunday, when I was a child of seven, we attended our first picnic at the new Episcopal church. I didn't want to play with the other children, boys mostly, already dirty from dabbling at the edge of the creek that ran by the churchyard. Mother forced me, pushing my narrow, hunched up shoulders into the sunny field crawling with the dark shapes of children.

One of the girls approached me, hesitantly asked my name. I barely whispered, "Edwina." A know-nothing boy who'd hidden behind a nearby bush, yelled at the top of his frenzied lungs "Edwee-wee!" The adults had, by this time, gathered around the picnic tables and were in the process of preparing the food. There was no one, not even my little brother, George, to help me.

Soon, all the wicked little boys were screeching about my

name and various bodily functions. I won't repeat all that was said.

I simply stood there, motionless and silent, until the horrible monsters lost interest in plaguing me. The girls, shocked by my lack of violence against the naughty fellows who were their brothers and friends, left me alone. That was the beginning of my social life in Charleston. Oh, I did receive party invitations after the horrid event. Mother saw to that. After all, we were wealthy, even richer than the aristocracy of the South. Money can take one a long way. Perhaps not everywhere, but almost.

I knew then, at that tender age, the awesome power of language. Though words broke no bones, they could surely hurt you. And I began to dwell on my name.

Not that Edwina is the only name with its future held in the syllables. Take Jack. Jack Sprat, Jack Frost, Jack... well, decorum forbids it. Oh, Jack's the name of a rake, a rogue, a little white-headed boy with a wide grin, who'd steal your lunch the minute your back is turned.

I loved a Jack once. He stood outside the marketplace on a frosty morning. I noticed him right away, though I was supposed to be choosing the sweet potatoes for our upcoming Thanksgiving meal. Usually, the cook, Hesperus, did our marketing, but Mother always insisted that for special occasions, I would oversee Cook's business. Mother knew that anyone with a name like Hesperus couldn't be trusted on holidays.

Jack wore a blue silk cravat at his throat and his shirt had tiny tucks across the front like a wedding shirt. His suit, black and expensive, fit him well and showed off his squarish body, the thick muscled body of a fighter or a man who labored outside at a job that called for strength.

He didn't fidget but simply waited until Cook and I carried our bundles out the front door.

" 'Scuse me, ma'am. You look like you might need a little help with those. May I?" He already had relieved me of my package and was in the process of claiming one of Cook's. She didn't relinquish hers so easily.

"I manage myself, thank you." Her entire tone asked, 'Who he think he is, talking straight out to Miss Edwina, right here on the street?' At that moment, I felt an undeniable fondness for Cook, though usually I resented our joint errands.

I stared into Jack's pure blue eyes and said, "It's all right, Cook. This gentleman only wishes to assist us and I'm sure meant no harm." I smiled at him with as much warmth as I could muster and hoped it would be enough.

Immediately, he asked my name and before I had a chance to consider, I'd blurted out the truth. An error. If only I'd answered Suzanne or Catherine, names with regal bearing and beauty. I could almost see his disappointment when my mouth formed the *-weee* part of the second syllable, that long E whistling across my windpipes like the screech of an unsightly starling.

When he'd given me his *Jack*, my heart pumped quickly. It was a fast name, one that promised adventure, maybe even danger. One beat and it was over—a single syllable you could spit out in anger or gasp in passion. The thought made me blush and I was glad. At least I wouldn't seem so pale in the November air.

Along the several blocks to the waterfront and my home, I discovered much about my Jack.

"Where are you from, Mr. Applewhite?" His surname, not the least bit aristocratic, was so unlike my own, Carruthers, a title of bluest blood. I rather enjoyed the difference. And he was unusual as well, nothing like the slender young men I saw escorting debutantes, boys little used to physical labor, but accustomed to leisure and plenty.

"West Virginia. I'm in the coal industry. Came south on business." West Virginia was an inappropriate state, I knew, but, though his manners weren't as smooth as those of Charleston boys, he tried to show his civil acumen. Besides, his voice was so manly, a deep baritone with a bit of gravel in it, that I began to thrill to the sound and walked more closely than was quite proper. He noticed and his arm brushed mine on more than one occasion.

"How long will you be staying?" It was an innocent question, I thought. Nothing indecent about such a general interrogation.

"Several months, I hope. Long enough to become a friend to the South." He looked directly at me, as though I represented that friend he wished to make.

"Tell me, how does a lovely woman such as yourself find entertainment here?" Not a single soul had ever called me lovely before. And I knew, from hours of prayer at my looking-glass, that, indeed, I was not lovely. But hearing him say it made me hope it was true.

"Well, there are lots of parties, cotillions. And of course the symphony..." I chattered away as if I were privy to these social gatherings. Yes, I'd attended, but always in the company of my parents, never with a young man or a group of friends my own age. For a woman of twenty-five, I'm certain that must have been some kind of record.

I'll never forget the walk that day. Though it was November, the air was somewhat warm and there were a few bright leaves scattered among the tree limbs. The water, green like the underbelly of our local lizards, was calm, serene.

Or maybe the day was cold, the wind a whip to us, forcing us to huddle together. The waves rose and fell like heavy breath and before I knew it, I'd asked Sweet Jack in for some hot tea. I knew Mother would be shocked at such a brazen move on my part, but I didn't care. Nor did I mind that Jack was an outsider. It was, after all, the Twentieth Century. In 1912, an invitation to tea must be allowed. Progress, after all.

I knew what Mother would say to my arguments. "Just because things change, doesn't make forward behavior right. You'll see. Decency will always be decency."

Mother counted everything by such rules. And by names. The stores she frequented, the goods she purchased, the street she lived on—Darlington Avenue, in the heart of the wealthy section—Mother chose as a result of the name. I, too, took notice of such things, but for different reasons.

"Delighted." Mother's only comment to Jack that afternoon, delivered in a voice that predicted the cold of the coming winter.

"You have a lovely home, Mrs. Carruthers." He tried every tack the poor man's brain could think of. Nothing worked. Mother soon left us to our tea, her 'MMmm' lingering in the air, wrapping us together against the chill she left behind.

After that first day, Jack and I met frequently, always uptown. I concocted a thousand reasons to shop and Mother didn't bat an eye when I insisted on planning our menus for the Yuletide celebrations. I chose recipes clipped from the society page of our paper. These called for exotic items which Cook and I searched for relentlessly.

What Mother didn't know was that I'd leave Cook to shop while I walked down stretches of cobbled roads, mud byways, rutted routes and woodsy paths. I kept to the clean side of town at first, followed street names I knew well. Often I'd meet Jack on these thoroughfares by secret arrangement. We'd stroll together, me on important business and Jack for the pleasure of my company. So he told me.

But before I realized, I began to drift over to the other sections of town on my daily outings. The wharves and seedier places where the stench of commerce hung on the air, where everything was for sale at one price or another. The first time

Jack took me to these dark, dangerous streets, I considered racing home, back to the world I knew, a world with rules. But it didn't take long for him to convince me that life held more than rules.

Once I saw a woman dressed in what must have been the most lewd underskirts I'd ever seen. She waved at Jack almost as if she knew him. He kept his eyes on me, however, and didn't seem to notice her at all. It's my belief she was a woman of ill repute. The thought excited me in a way I couldn't quite fathom. I enjoyed meandering through these low sections, safe on Jack's sturdy arm. I became an explorer of sorts, making forays into forbidden territory, the way I imagined men of Jack's caliber might venture without fear to new places.

I watched street signs, not for directions, but for clues. Regis Park had such a lovely sound, like a fine place where they served meals, even breakfast, with the good silver. In reality, the road itself was of sand and soot, and my boots had to be cleaned for three hours to remove all evidence of my journey according to Cook, who never uttered a word of complaint over her extra, clandestine duties.

Then there was Market Street, a place that implied noise and bustling business. Another lie. It was a narrow, one-lane gully that led past the stockyards to the river. As I made these discoveries, I began to look for such incongruities in human names. I'd discovered that though called 'Edwina,' I had the heart of a Gwendolyn, a passionate nature that enjoyed stealing away into the nether parts of Charleston. A woman accompanied was allowed access to the entire city, where a woman alone...well, no decent woman would stroll by herself in such places.

Sometimes on our excursions, I had hints about how I'd appear at mid-life, Edwina Carruthers, a clumsiness having taken over my youthful temerity, my gait like that of a broken mule. These visions were triggered by the sight and sound of a particularly unattractive person of mean circumstances, male or female, young or old. Then I'd force myself to consider the passion I felt, my secret 'Gwendolyn' nature. Perhaps I'd become one of those lush women, full and earthy, who are able to wear their womanhood like a mantle of ermine, soft and elegant. Or, if my name were Edwina Applewhite? The sound of it was too much to be imagined and I could get no image, none at all.

Such thoughts, dark and cloudy, didn't matter, though, because Jack would meet me and distract me from my considerations. Together we would walk in the last moments before dark, those rosy minutes when the sun hit the painted wrought iron fence behind my house and turned it a rosy vermilion.

Even my face took on the peachy glow of sunset, and it was then that Jack ventured to kiss me as we stood down by the boat docks.

Or the day might have been stormy, the wind a robber stealing warmth, turning our mouths filmy with the cold. Blue-lipped, face the color of thin, gray clouds, Jack at my elbow, I was never kissed, but rather skated around the town, gliding, the hem of my dress catching on the rough sidewalk boards at the harbor.

Jack told me all about the mountains of West Virginia and how he'd become involved in the mining industry. Without actually saying so, he indicated he had attended West Point.

"I enjoyed my military service, Miss Carruthers. And, were it not for my clumsily flat feet, I might have continued it." He always called me Miss Carruthers, though he knew my given name. I knew he couldn't bear the sound of it, didn't want to assault the air with its ugly implications. And I always addressed him as Mr. Applewhite. We were, after all, not betrothed. We were walking partners.

I could see Jack in my mind's eye, crisp and starched in his uniform, the younger soldiers calling him 'sir.' Oh, how I longed to become something more to him than his South Carolina friend. How I wished to be on his arm at important gatherings, business meetings that might change the course of our very own South. I wanted to be dressed in the finest silks and satins. I could, after all, afford such luxuries. Only my linsey-woolsey name kept me from the fabrics most women of my station wore with enjoyment. After all, what would Uncle Edward have thought about such indulgences? And how could I feel the smooth fabric against my skin without flinching at the rough sound of my own name?

I knew I'd never be anything beyond Edwina for Jack. Even my middle name, Jane, wouldn't serve to distinguish me. Jack deserved an Estelle or a Colette.

Imagine my chagrin when he didn't seem to understand our obvious positions. Truth be told, I couldn't imagine myself with a Jack, no matter how bright his future looked, no matter the allure of his masculine voice. There's something missing in the name, a lack of trustworthiness that I could see for myself. I didn't need Mother's constant reminding.

"Edwina, I've discovered with whom you take your walks, my dear. I must warn you, there's something about Mr. Applewhite... the garish way his ears stick out. You can't trust a man who looks so comical from behind. I won't forbid you to see him, but I will surely disinherit you if anything untoward happens."

Where Mother saw deformity, I saw beauty. The wide expanse of cartilage between the rim of his ear and his head seemed to me the perfect place to kiss or run over with the tip of one's tongue. Such thoughts shocked me and I knew they sprang from that other nature, the Gwendolyn, a woman capable of who-knew-what. Mother's sermon didn't tell me one thing I couldn't have already guessed. Jack was so handsome, so charming, women would never leave him alone. And I sometimes doubted his purity of motive. The idea that he might be interested in me for investment purposes had occurred. But I never dwelt on it.

On the night, or was it morning, that he proposed, the moon was a sliver, a pale C against the dark heavens. The spring night air was cool, but clear, and I could see the stars, bright pinpricks of light scattered across the dusky sky. The ocean itself was subdued and quiet. We stood under the weeping willow tree in the garden behind my house. His eyes, intelligent, but gentle, seemed to plead for understanding and affection. A shock of blond hair fell across his wide forehead and there, in the late evening, he seemed to be more than he actually was—a pirate, a gambler, a spy. Unfortunately, I was exactly what I was, Edwina.

He took my gloved hand in his own squarish one, cupped it gently, like my fingers were made of porcelain. He kissed them one by one, the warmth of his lips burning through the material. His eyes didn't leave my face and I could feel myself sinking, sinking down into the mist that rose off the water. I'd give myself to him; there was not one doubt. Marry up with him, though I could see there'd be nothing but trouble. A country bumpkin really, that's all he was in spite of his varnish of etiquette. Jack Applewhite. Humph. A name common as chicken feed.

Yet, I could have taken his name, woven my initials with his on our monogrammed linens. I could have, but instead I sealed our fates.

His voice was all atremble. "Edie, would you consider marrying me?"

Edie! He'd never hinted that he thought of me that way. The huskiness of the repeated 'E' sound, low and rather desperate, made me quiver. Some force took hold of me, some ancient thing. I threw my arms around his thick neck.

"Call me Edie again. Say it, Jack, say it." The growl that tore from his throat terrified me, yet I found myself kissing him, allowing him to touch me, lift my skirts. We fell together under the willow tree, hidden from my house, Mother becoming a part of the shadows.

Or perhaps there was no riotous behavior in the darkened grass. Instead, he simply fell to one knee, tucked his hat under his arm and made his request.

"Now will you marry me, Edwina Jane Carruthers?" His voice sounded confident, a slight derisive emphasis on the last two syllables of my first name. Or so I thought. He kept talking but I didn't hear anything after he'd called me by my full name. In those few syllables, I heard my whole life pass in one long moment. Edwina Jane couldn't marry, wouldn't take a man into her bedroom. Not nightly. Not to be defiled on a regular basis. She hadn't the nerve to slip under the covers wearing no undergarments, an Edwina couldn't stand the passion of such nights. She'd burn up as quickly as pine needles in autumn. No, Edwina Jane sat alone in the library reading Sonnets to the Portuguese, dreaming of Robert Browning—a stalwart name—just the sort of man who might steal her away. The fire lit her white features, ruddied up her sunken cheeks and cast hints of gold in her eyes.

Edwina Jane dared not bear the consequence of children, a bloody reminder of joined names. No child would want an Edwina for a mother, a woman cold and hard, with bony places in her heart. And what family heirloom could Jack give the hybrids he might spawn? Applewhite? It sounded like a kind of whiskey.

The silence of the next few moments was loud as the squall of the sea. Jack tried to force me to look at him, but after my complete display of myself, I dared not. He kept talking, his voice sad and low. He seemed at odds, not quite knowing what to do. I stared out upon the water, said nothing, did not move, barely breathed. I lost track of time, could only note the rise of the moon as it lifted, like a sickle, across the heavens.

Finally, Jack took my arm and led me to our parlor door. I saw Mother staring out the bay window in the dining room, a gray shape behind the curtain. I continued my silence, refused to utter a word. I could hear the waves and the sound was like a voice, a soft something calling. I could only sigh and mouth "Mrs. Jack Applewhite" over and over, my face hidden under a winter bonnet, the wool of the brim sturdy against the biting wind.

Though I mouthed the words, I knew they would never become real. I would refuse Jack, had already turned against him. Any man who could sway me the way he had, who could think of me as 'Edie'—such a man was dangerous.

How Dare These Women in My Bed

David M. Shaw

There are women in my bed from all walks of life. Latino, Thai, African, Indian. Sweet Mulatto mixes, thin-necked Brits and Swedes. A former star of the opera and a second-rate actress of the film. A jockey, a rocket scientist, a zookeeper, a bookkeeper, an entirely disgruntled beekeeper. Also, two strippers and a Pulitzer Prize Winner. It's so damn crowded the springs are giving out. The sheets are filthy. Everybody has an attitude.

"We can all please you," the naked women sing in the darkness. "Let us give you what you want."

How dare these women in my bed insist that they can satisfy me? At night I fight sleep in the little corner of the bed they assign me, until one of them starts running her nails against my back, and then they all are awake, pawing over me, owning my poor, overtaxed, clotheless body.

"Everybody out," I finally say one night.

I close my eyes and imagine them all picking up their clothes off the floor, kimonos and headwraps and brassieres, and putting them on for the first time in forever.

"Do you really mean everybody?" they ask.

"Everybody," I say. "That goes for you supermodels, too."

"But——" they try.

"No buts," I say. "Please just leave."

There are a few knowing sighs, as if I have forgotten something.

"And take your lipsticks."

An hour of elastic-slapping and more sighing, and finally they are gone. I, of course, still am sleepless. I watch the moon through the window. I hear for the first time in months the waves crashing shore. I venture outside into the cold silver air.

You know the rest.

The moon sets. The waves calm. The breeze passes away into night. There's me, racing home to bed again, then feeling through the dark for leftover panties or shoes or mascara. Anything.

Siren's Voices

MariJo Moore

Siren could hear voices. At the age of seven she heard the voice of one of the Old Ones whisper in her ear, "Go and tell your mama to stop messing around with that judge." Siren knew it was the voice of one of the Old Ones because of the smell that circled the voice. It was the smell of the aged. The voice smelled just like the faded photographs her Aunt Lucille kept in a tattered cigar box underneath her bed.

Siren hid underneath this bed whenever her Aunt Lucille and Uncle Jeb fought, and they fought quite a bit around Jeb's payday. She and her mother had left the mountains of East Tennessee and gone to live with her mother's older sister in the western part of the state when Siren was just a baby. Her daddy had died in a hunting accident (more like a drunken brawl she had heard her mama say several times), and so her young mother was left to fend for herself and her baby. The tiny turquoise house belonged to her Aunt Lucille, the cramped living situation adding to the aggravation of the family.

"Who is this woman right here? The one holding the baby?" Siren asked one Saturday afternoon after a loud screaming match between her aunt and uncle. Jeb had slammed the screen door behind him proclaiming, as usual, that it would be a cold day in hell before his shadow would be racing home to darken the inside of this crazy house again.

"He'll be back when he gets horny," Siren heard her Aunt Lucille mutter underneath her breath. She was standing at the sink in their skinny kitchen, peeling potatoes and whistling something that sounded like "When The Saints Go Marching In." Lucille had had the great fortune of attending Mardi Gras down in New Orleans when she was a teenager. All that saintly music had etched a furrow in her brain in which no other type of music could ever grow, no matter what she tried to plant there. No matter if she listened to Pat Boone singing "Love Letters in The Sand" fifty times a day, she still woke up with the sound of Fats Domino singing "I'm Walking To New Orleans" coming from her whistle box, as she liked to call it.

"I said, Aunt Lucille, 'Who is this?' "

"Now where did you get that?" Lucille's voice rose to the ceiling and bounced back atop Siren's head.

"I found it."

"Found it where?" Lucille's eyes narrowed and reminded Siren of a snake she had seen in a Tarzan movie the week before.

"Found it out in the yard, laying right next to that old John Deere tractor sitting next to the barn." Siren not only heard voices, she also lied a lot.

"That's one of them old pictures I keep underneath my bed, now ain't it? What are you doing under there? Look at you! Dust balls all in your hair! That's your old granny's granny and you should have more respect than to go messing around in other people's things. Go put it back! Now!"

"She talked to me this morning." Siren said this matter-of-factly, just as she would have said, "It's stopped raining."

Her aunt stopped peeling and looked her dead in the eyes.

"What do you mean, she talked to you this morning?"

"I knew it was one of the Old Ones talking to me because the voice smelled just like all those old photographs underneath your bed. So I just had to see which one it was, and I'm pretty sure it was this one. What's her name? She's Indian like us, ain't she?"

"You never mind what's her name or what she is! And you quit lying, you sharped-tongued, nosy youngun! You march your little butt right back in there and put it right back where you found it! I'll tell your mama when she gets home and she'll whip your little butt for real!"

This threat didn't scare Siren because she knew it would be late when her mama got home. She was out with the judge and they had probably gone over to St. Louis or somewhere where they thought no one would recognize them. Like no one would pay any attention to a fat old balding judge and a beautiful raven-haired young woman hugging and kissing on each other. And besides, whenever her mama came home late, she slept most of the next day, and more than likely Aunt Lucille would have forgotten about the entire incident by then.

The voice of one of the Old Ones whispered once more as Siren pulled the tattered cigar box from beneath the bed, "Be sure and tell your mama to stop messing around with that judge."

When Siren told her mama what the voice of the one of the Old Ones had whispered in her ear, her mama eyed her suspiciously and then announced in a voice that was heard by the cotton pickers working in the field just down the road, "Well, it's none of your business or anybody else's what I do! And you quit listening to them voices! You hear me? And stop that damn lying!"

But Siren continued to listen to the voices, partly because she liked to listen to them and partly because she didn't like her mama very much.

When Siren was eleven, she found the epic poem "The

Odyssey" written by the poet Homer in a library book at school. When she returned home that afternoon, her mama was lying outside in the sun, trying to sweat the beer from the night before out of her system. Siren sat down next to her and began sipping on lemonade her Aunt Lucille had left for her in the skinny kitchen.

"Mama, by any chance did you at one time read 'The Odyssey' by Homer? You know, the long poem about Odysseus on his way home from theTrojan War? This mythical monster, half woman and half bird, tries to lure his ship full of men over to the rocks where they will crash. Her name was Siren. Is that where you got the idea for my name?" Siren knew she was going out on a limb asking this. She had never seen her mama read anything except *True Confessions* and *TV Guide* occasionally to see if any Clark Gable movies were coming on television the nights the judge couldn't get away from his wife.

"Naw, I never read that," her copper-faced mother said between juicy chews of gum. "I named you Siren 'cause I heard one siren after the other going off the night your daddy made love to me over and over 'til he was sure I was pregnant. There musta been a huge fire or robbery or somethin' somewhere in town 'cause them sirens went off all night long."

Shortly after this revelation, Siren began wearing a white tablecloth over her head when she was at home. When asked why, she would explain in a low, dramatic voice, "Because I don't exist. I am a ghost. The ghost of a noise heard by my mama as she slept with my daddy so many years ago. I am a ghost who doesn't exist."

"Well, for a ghost who don't exist, you sure make one helluva mess," her Aunt Lucille said. "Just look at that jelly and peanut butter glopped all over my kitchen chairs!"

"Siren, take that damn thing off your head!" Her mama had tired of this drama after about three days. "Come on, now," her voice softened as she remembered that Judge Ripley was due to come over that evening and she didn't want Siren to embarrass her any more than usual. "Let that beautiful black hair show! You know that black curly hair is the richest thing your daddy could have ever given you."

Siren took the tablecloth off her head. The next day she took her Uncle Jeb's white shoe polish and painted her onyx curls white. When her mama saw this, she made her sit outside in the rain until all the white washed off. "What are them voices saying to you now, Miss Smartie Pants?" her mama asked as Siren came inside, white streaks covering her whole body. "Are they telling you not to be so damned stupid?"

Siren began to tell bigger lies. No one noticed. Siren shaved off one of her eyebrows. No one noticed. Siren cut off her bangs. No one noticed. Siren took a double-edged blade from her Uncle Jeb's razor and sliced the inside of her left arm. They noticed.

"I guess them silly-ass voices told you to do this, eh?" Uncle Jeb didn't speak much unless he felt like he had something of importance to say or he was watching wrestling on television. He yelled quite a bit then. Sometimes Siren thought the man actually believed all that stuff was real. He had taken Siren to the emergency room at the local hospital where a stringy-looking intern had sewn the flesh of her arm back together.

"Naw, they don't tell me to do bad things to myself. They just tell me things about people. Like for instance, last week, a voice that smelled like popcorn told me that you got several bottles of Jack Daniels stashed out in the barn."

Jeb almost ran the car off the road. "You been watching me?" His upper lip began to sweat. He knew if Lucille found out about those bottles she wouldn't let him have any spending money come Saturday night.

"Naw, I got better things to do than follow you around."

"Yeah, like slice away at your arm."

For the next two years, Siren spoke to her family only out of necessity. Mostly she just read, sat in her room, and listened to the voices. Soon she was able to hear conversations between people who were miles away. She also began to read the thoughts of others. After her thirteenth birthday (her mama and the judge gave her a record player and her aunt and uncle gave her a bracelet with ugly charms attached), Siren began taking long walks at night and thinking about how it must feel to be free of thoughts. How wonderful it would be to not have to think—to not have to listen to the voices that told her things she really didn't want to know. Like how her history teacher, Mr. Walden, was diddling her gym teacher, Miss Nichols. Or about how Harry Jenkins, the town's most prominent banker, was stealing money from his patrons right and left.

When Siren was sixteen, a voice with no odor came to her and said, "Run away from home."

"Tell me, where's your smell?" Siren didn't trust voices with no smell. She was now full of piss and vinegar, as her mama liked to say, and wasn't afraid to talk back to anyone or anything, especially the voices.

"Run away from these crazy people, I tell you, or you'll be sorry."

"Nope. Not 'til you let me smell your smell. I don't listen to voices that don't smell."

"Suit yourself," the odorless voice said.

THE RAIN
by Siren

Thanks for the rain
the beautiful falling silver rain.
Give us a strong storm of consolation
strong beating winds of affirmation

tiny, tiny drops of tantamount receptions
and a pot to piss in.

Rain rain rain down like a son-of-a-bitch
scattering lightning and
scaring us all into asking deeper
questions of our intentions.

Clamoring down
down down
like a whore on a hundred dollar bill
or a baby after a new thought.

At this time in her life, Siren began writing poetry. Some of
the writings were her own ideas, but mostly she wrote what the
voices told her to write. She liked to think that one of them
might be William Faulkner because it always smelled like whiskey
and said things like "clamoring down like a whore on a hundred
dollar bill."

"Now, she's not only hearing voices, lying a lot, slicing away at
herself, but writing nasty poetry too!" her mama screamed when
she was snooping through Siren's closet one day looking for a pair
of shoes to borrow. "Y'all come in here and look at this! She's
writing nasty poetry!"

"I told you to run away," the odorless voice said.

Three months before her graduation from high school, Siren
was watching television and dreaming of the new boy who had
just moved to town when she heard someone pull into the
driveway. She was home alone and thought it must be a salesman
or maybe the Combine Insurance man come to collect her Aunt
Lucille's premium for the month. But when she looked outside,
the sheriff's car, looking menacing yet protective, had stopped just
three feet from the tiny turquoise house. Sheriff Tom, all six-feet-

three-inches of him, came to the front door. "Where's your aunt and uncle, Missy?"

"They've gone into town shopping. What's wrong?" Siren knew something bad was going to happen because all morning a voice that smelled like a funeral parlor kept whispering in her ear, "She didn't do it. Tell them she didn't do it."

"Well, it seems somebody's done gone and whacked off the top of Judge Ripley's head. And your mama — now we don't know for sure she did it — but your mama has been arrested for the murder. She's the one who called us to come down to the S&S Motel over on Highway 20. Lord, it was a mess in that room! Looked like somebody been killin' hogs in there."

Siren's sharp tongue climbed to the roof of her mouth and refused to come down. Her mama? Arrested for murdering the judge? Why, she loved that old Coot!

"I reckon it's best you stay here. I'll go and try to find Lucille and Jeb and see if they want to get your mama a lawyer. I wouldn't answer the phone or door if I was you. The townsfolk are pretty upset about this whole thing." He spat tobacco juice into Lucille's tulip bed and then left.

Siren's tongue climbed down from the roof of her mouth even before the car had pulled out of the driveway. "What am I going to do?" Where were the voices now that she needed them? "I said, what am I going to do?"

"I told you to run away from home," the odorless voice said. "I told you to tell her to stop messing with that judge," the voice of one of the Old Ones said. "I told you she didn't do it," the funeral parlor voice said.

"Dammit! One of you with some sense come and tell me what to do!" A wisp of Brylcream entered the living room.

"Sit down," the Brylcream voice said. This was a voice of authority. This was a voice she intuitively recognized. This was the voice of her dead daddy.

"Get a piece of paper and write this down. I'll tell you exactly what you are to do."

When Siren's mama went to trial for the murder of Judge Ripley, the whole town was there. Those who couldn't squeeze into the tiny courthouse were outside on the steps, screaming things like "Murderer! Adulteress! Shameless Indian Whore Hussy!" Siren ignored them as she walked into the courtroom and handed the bailiff an envelope. He opened the envelope and read what was scribbled on several sheets of notebook paper. His face turned a bright red. Swallowing hard and trying to regain his composure, he neatly put the pages back inside the envelope and then handed it to the presiding judge who was just entering the courtroom. The presiding judge's face turned a pale shade of green as he read what Siren had written. He then whispered into the bailiff's ear and Siren was brought to the presiding judge's chambers.

"Young lady, where did you get this?" The presiding judge was trying to maintain an air of dignity though his hands were shaking uncontrollably.

"I wrote it."

"Where did you get the information you wrote?" His voice was now shaking as badly as his hands.

"I hear voices. A voice that smelled like Brylcream told me to write those things down and give them to you the day of my mama's trial. That's my mama out there who is being accused of a murder she didn't commit."

The presiding judge looked at the bailiff. "She's got times and dates and places," he whispered loudly. His body was beginning to show stains of sweat through the dark robe.

"I know. I read it," the bailiff answered in an even louder whisper.

"What do you plan to do with this, young lady? You know you could ruin the lives of some very important people in this town." And to the bailiff, "If my wife finds out about us, she'll nail my ass to the wall!" The bailiff shook his head in agreement and looked at Siren with pleading in his eyes.

"I thought I might sell it to you. But if you're not interested, I'm sure somebody down at the newspaper might want to see it."

"How much, I mean, what do you mean, sell it to me?"

"Well, I know and you know that my mama didn't kill Judge Ripley. I know and you know that his crazy, jealous wife is the one that chopped off the top of his head. But I know and you know that you ain't about to arrest her because her family owns half this county. So, I figure if you get my mama off, let her go free, then I'll sell you that information and call it an even trade."

"And you wouldn't tell anyone else?"

"Naw, I'd sign something swearing to that. I know you like to sleep nights, just like everybody else. And I know you wouldn't want everyone knowing just how close you two are." She eyed the bailiff accusingly.

Two weeks later, Siren, her Aunt Lucille, Uncle Jeb, and her mama sat in their back yard drinking lemonade. "I'm so grateful to be free of that damn jail!" Her mama spoke between sips of lemonade and drags of Viceroy. "And I owe it all to my sweet little Siren."

"You never did tell us what you told that presiding judge." Her Aunt Lucille looked at Siren from behind mirrored sunglasses.

"Naw, and I ain't about to."

Seven months after Siren's mama was released from the murder on a technicality (it seems the arresting policeman had forgotten to read her her rights) she was killed while helping a new boyfriend rob a bank. She stopped breathing as soon as the bullet bit into her heart.

Siren was enjoying a full-paid scholarship, compliments of the presiding judge, at the University of Arizona at Tuscon when she heard the news. "I told you to run away from home," the odorless voice said. "I told you to tell her to stop messing with that judge," the voice of one of the Old Ones said. "I told you she didn't do it," the funeral parlor voice said. "I told you it would all work out this way," the Brylcream voice said.

"And I told all of you we'd eventually go to Europe with the insurance money, now didn't I?" Siren screamed at them, silencing the voices, for at least a little while.

Housecleaning

Val Nieman

Nan Vogelsang spent evenings and weekends cleaning up what he left behind.

He left on a Tuesday and never looked back, let the attorneys handle it. Of course, they never visited the dim half-finished basement to cart out the board-ends and old lumber, glue gone bad in the tube, carpet squares, wire nuts, a rake without a handle, loose Allen wrenches, a hacksaw with the blade worked beyond its usefulness. None of this was mentioned in the legal documents.

Or the nails bent in driving them, thrown back in the blue cardboard boxes along with the good ones. Pounds of nails, spikes and finishing nails, roofing nails and decking nails. More than anything else, nails.

And the sandpaper discs, clotted with blackened shellac. An old picture frame, come apart at opposite corners into two right angles. A pair of shears, rusted. Washers. Stove bolts. A can opener with grease on the handle. The start of a butcher-block table top, the edges raw and top unfinished. Sockets loose from their set. A gallon of neat's-foot oil. PVC joints. Brick-colored rags tossed under the workbench. A square of plexiglass. WD-40. The kitchen wall clock that buzzed and stuck. A broken kite. A wall calendar from the gas station. A Phillips-head screwdriver with a broken tip, used for mixing and prying, the end gobbed with tar. Flux and a roll of solder and the torch but no propane. Paint sticks. Sawdust pushed aside by his hand.

He was gone gone gone. To another life, like a cicada coming up out of the ground after nine years. That was how he'd explained things to a friend, who by way of other friends brought the story back around to her.

He was flown, she thought, or crawled away, but the discarded shell remained. And it was supposed to be seventeen years.

She couldn't see how the marriage had been cut off so abruptly; neither could she project ahead the time they might have spent together. The years fell away to both sides. All she could see, if things had not changed, for more years, or ever, was that eventually they would have been swamped with the accumulation of George's things. And maybe that's why he left, she thought as she filled another box. Rusted trowel. Wood putty. One glove with the thumb broken through. He wasn't able to deal with the complexity of the accumulated and undiscarded.

She thought it was his upbringing; his parents, country people who got factory jobs but continued to live on acreage they rented to people who milked cattle and grew corn. You didn't throw things away that might be used for propping or filling, holding or patching. It was a useful trait among farm people, like those whose rotting fences had been cut across by the lot lines in this subdivision. In the suburbs, a habit of saving things was like an appendix, or tonsils, without purpose, only problematic.

A round red reflector disc, the glue on the back gone brittle. A chunk of two-by-four. Electrical tape. Handles from an old filing cabinet.

Nan had never intruded on his shop. She knew how he

worked, everything strung out across the workbench, and anything picked up or moved could set a project back for hours, or forever. The sheer number of things here had put her off for months, while she'd soldiered through the financial shifts and legal matters. She donated sporting goods to the Scouts, tools to the shelter workshop. She'd carted his abandoned clothes to the Goodwill, lowering the bags into the drop-off bin and then racing home, hoping people in the shopping center believed her to be a young widow.

She pulled out a coffee can with a trim brush dried to the bottom, tossed it in the box. This disorder was so much a part of him that, with George gone, the vitality was gone, too. There'd been a hopefulness in his hoarding.

Nan hefted the box and climbed the basement stairs, threw her hip against the door to hold it open while she shifted the box across to the cargo deck of the van backed close against the house. She pushed the box against the others already there. At her feet, the grass showed need of cutting.

She brushed flakes of rust from her hands, went back down and started on the paint cans. She shook each one in turn, some of the gallons so light that they swung high in the air when she pulled them from under the workbench. There were pint cans of stain they had moved from their last house, now thick as syrup. Finally, she went down on one knee to peer under the bench, finding dust, a spool of string for the weed-whacker, and a dead cricket.

What was that? She reached with a yardstick and scraped at something black on the wall. Nothing moved. It wasn't an insect or spider. Nan poked her head into the recess.

The back of the workbench had a scrap of flakeboard nailed against the uprights to keep cans from sliding off the shelves. The rough surface was scrawled with black china marker, columns of large figures in George's familiar handwriting. Sevens that looked like ones, all the numbers slewing with the lope of a bear on a downslope, gaining speed.

Nan took hold of the board and yanked. It creaked against the nails that held it. She squatted and put both hands to the board, pulled steadily. The flakeboard groaned and then gave all at once, and she went half onto her back, rocked forward with the piece of board in her hands. The edges were splintered where compressed fragments of wood broke apart under pressure. She rolled to her knees, her head thrust forward under the workbench, and saw the place the board had been. The bare block wall was visible now, dull gray like something dead, like a bad tooth. Like the socket where a bad tooth has been removed.

She tossed the board into the garbage box. The figures slanted across. Calculations for 2-by-4s, how many needed on 16-inch centers. Nan remembered the trucks from the lumberyard stacked with framing lumber and plywood.

Nan turned the board over, carried the box to the van. She slammed the liftgate down. In the morning, she'd drive by the landfill and dispose of the mess.

But in bed that night, she kept seeing the scrawled numbers. Her skin itched, like after sunburn, like there'd been too much bleach in the wash. Like columns of ants adding toward some subterranean explosion.

*   *   *

The next morning, Nan went down to the workshop and began pulling tools from their wall hooks. Crowbar, pliers, a claw hammer with the cracked handle mended by duct tape. She swung the crowbar as she climbed the stairs, liking the heft of it, recalling through her skin how steel warmed to the hand, how wood handles felt oily from long use. Not since they built the place had Nan used tools in earnest — only for picture-hanging, or once, assembling a bed frame.

She knew there were other scribblings, curses cut into the memory of the house. Behind the wallpaper. On the joists under her feet and the rafters above. Nan stood in the living room. She didn't need to close her eyes to make the furniture disappear and the lamps and books, the barnboard paneling.

He's standing by the rough opening for the patio door, turned away from her after she'd failed at something he asked. The baggy seat of his jeans is dusty. He clenches a flat carpenter's pencil, maroon, the soft lead sharpened by a knife, and draws lines backward in that graceless left-hand style.

Nan put the flat prongs of the crowbar under a board. She leaned her weight against the curved opposite end. The gray board, though pocked with nail-holes and cracked by long-ago weather, was strong and popped its nails, one two three. She pried up the other end, then opened the sliding glass door and flung the board across the deck and onto the lawn.

The barnboard paneling was laid up in diagonal rows that met in the middle like sergeant's stripes. She pulled the boards free on one side from waist height to the ceiling, then started on the opposite row.

She was halfway up that side when the first marks appeared, a rough sketch of a door or window, and words. The names of suppliers? She couldn't tell, the letters illegible. On the dented white surface of the sheetrock, they looked like the scrawl of a ransom note, a threat wrapped around a brick and thrown through a window.

She pried up board after board, each a satisfying yield, and tossed them with a harvester's economy of motion out the door.

The arrival of a car would have gone unnoticed except that the neighbor's dog began to bark and gallop from corner to corner of his invisible fence. Nan quit work, heard the momentary race of a car engine being put into park. She went to the front door.

Dave Oliver's red pickup was in the drive, and he was at the bottom of the stairs, looking up at her, one foot on the step, one on the ground.

"Hey, Nan." He paused. "I was on my way to the home center."

He looked at her strangely, his crooked mouth always on the verge of smile but now pulled down as though he might sob. She felt a flash of anger—am I that pitiful—then realized that she held the crowbar across her chest like a weapon. Sweat cooled on her temples and she felt the shine of exertion on her face, the blood pumping under her skin.

Dave looked past her into the house. She turned, saw the gutted wall.

"I'm getting rid of a few things," she said.

"Remodeling?"

"Just—getting rid." She swung the storm door wide. "Come on in."

He walked over to the wall, his hands shoved down in the pockets of his cut-off khakis, and gazed at the sheetrock. He tilted his head, trying to read.

"Y'know, I thought I was pretty close to George, as neighbors go," he said. "We did things together. He helped me build that fence. But I met him in town not long after he moved out, and he put his head down and walked by. Didn't say a word."

Dave turned, and his eyes were dry but that didn't signify a thing. "Whatever was between you two was just that. He had no reason to act like he did."

He held out his hand. Nan gave him the crowbar.

He drove the flat end under the drywall and pulled. The board cracked all the way across and gypsum trickled from the edge.

Her husband's friend broke out the section with the writing, then the part above and below. An eight-foot section of the stud wall stood open, with the pink insulation and the wiring snaking through holes in the 2-by-6s.

Nan threw the pieces into the backyard as he attacked the next section of paneling. Nails screeched. After a little while, Dave began to hum.

* * *

She was too tired to shower, throwing herself into bed coated with the chalk-tasting gypsum on her skin. She could smell mildew and the raw vinegar drench of wood wrenched apart.

Her body ached, her shoulders and thighs. She rolled from side to side. Her hair fell into her mouth, tasting foul, and she pulled it from her dry lips with dusty fingers.

Outside, crickets repeated things she would listen to, if she didn't respect herself more. They sawed and sawed, and late in the night a screech owl whinnied from a tree close by. George had left in late winter. It was summer. August.

Nan cried, the tears sliding silently down her face. The racking sobs that had left her breathless and strengthless had stopped, sometime in the spring.

She saw the living room wall, bare, and despaired of what she'd done. What was left to do.

After having avoided looking into them so long, she wasn't sure if she could take the comfort of people's eyes.

* * *

The next morning, Nan ate breakfast on the back patio, overlooking the pile of debris. Heavy dew had spotted the drywall. It beaded on a spider web strung between three angled boards.

She wasn't surprised to hear Dave's truck again. Whatever barrier there had been, whatever taboo or taint of uncleanness had clung to her abandonment, was broken. She was surprised, however, to see two other men crammed into the front seat of the Toyota.

"I brought help," Dave called.

"I see."

Rick had been another of her husband's neighborhood friends, from one street over, while Angelo made up the occasional foursome for golf or a bowling night. They nodded at her, stood with their hands on their hips, surveying the house, squinting against the sun that rested just above the ridgeline like a second horizon crossed that morning.

The men carried their own tools. Dave wore a leather belt with hangers, hammer, screwdrivers, pliers, nail-puller. Angelo had a Craftsman toolbox with drawers, and all the tools inside had red handles and were set into their proper places. Rick's tools slid and crashed inside the primer-gray metal box that was lid-sprung from some accident.

They started, though, by carrying all the living room furniture down into the yard. The leather couch, pole lamps, baskets. The recliner opened after they set it down, as though a family invisibly took its ease on the front lawn.

Dave set a boom box on the kitchen counter and Springsteen came full-throated from the speaker.

Down came the paneling, the rest of the weathered boards on the second side of the room. Then the drywall, bare or painted. The tools scraped and the men sang along with the parts of the songs they knew.

While they dismantled the living room, she started emptying the kitchen cupboards, climbing on the stepladder to reach far back on the upper shelves. Nan tossed down plastic butter tubs, picnic dishes, cracked cups. She found a Christmas plate deep in the back, forgotten, and set it in the sink.

The small cupboards over the refrigerator were hard to reach. That's where she found the red glass wine carafe received as a wedding gift, etched with roses and their initials, too gaudy for words. She scraped her arm against a raw edge, reaching for a set of spice jars still in their flimsy carton.

Nan sucked at the broken skin and welling blood. Her own salt taste was familiar, and the cutaneous heat of the scrape like all those bruises, cuts and splinters suffered in building this house with their own hands. Insulation had prickled in her skin for days after she stapled the pink batts into place. Grime caked inside her elbows. Spattered paint went unnoticed until Monday afternoon at her desk, when she bent to pick up a paper and saw the spray of fine white spots across her instep.

She had focused on the good ache of work, in her muscles and tendons, because the other ache couldn't be spoken of.

Nan could never tell if something was straight, the chalk lines climbing and diving away from her as she looked. It was a constant incapacity. If she anchored a tape measure, it twisted. If she hoisted a board, its weight slowly sank in her untrustworthy hands until his hammer drove the nail home with the edge just off plumb.

Harsh words drove her failure deep inside, until she didn't trust her body to move properly, until the evidence of her eyes couldn't be believed. Until she had to do things over and over, patting inanimate objects into place lest they move when she turned away.

The men ordered pizza for lunch, and she paid the girl who delivered it, and sat down cross-legged on the carpet to eat it right out of the box. Angelo did his Italian schtick. He had a thick neck but small, precise feet. Dave spun the three-legged stool that kept the lid from the cheese, making it clatter across the cardboard.

They moved to the kitchen. She moved to the guest bedroom. A twenty-year-old song came on the radio and she danced as she took down the curtains, lifting each hook from its slot in the traverse rod.

The men rolled away when the heat of the day was beginning to fade, the leaves on the maples spreading as the sun went down.

The living room was bare, a cell, clean as an excavation. Windows, studs, siding. The insulation had disappeared, and the wiring. The dining room was the same. In the kitchen, they had taken down the cupboards and removed the sheetrock, then pushed the appliances back into their places.

As the sun faded and the living room turned moon-colored with the glow of the streetlight through the bare windows, she went into the bath and ran a deep tub of steaming water. She poured herbal beads into the water. The back wall of the bathroom was the appliance wall of the kitchen; she could see the stamped steel and printed diagrams and coiled gas supply lines like organs through the framing.

Nan immersed her arms in the oil-filmed water, easing the scrapes and cuts. She squeezed out a sponge over the sore extent of a muscle. Her narrow knees flexed and extended like something remote and powerful.

Her skin shone. Shone like sweat. George had talked about sweat equity, his investment, recovering his investment.

She had made an investment, too. Now she was getting it back, a piece at a time.

She lay down in the bed, her skin smooth against the white sheets. She lay with arms outspread and legs apart, in the middle of the king-sized bed. Oil and herbs exuded from her skin, went deep into the linens, the image of her body radiating into the fabric, the heat of her body sealing a resinous imprint that would remain when she rose.

*   *   *

Nan used a pair of pliers to pull up the carpet.

The installers had stretched it across the floors and fastened it to narrow strips along the walls. The points of the tacks would prick her bare toes when she crossed a threshold or pressed her feet right up against the wall.

The carpet made a satisfying rip as she yanked it from its moorings. Dust that had seeped down over the years made little gray drifts along the strips. In some places the padding stuck to the underlayment. She remembered picking out this particular padding, not the very best but good, shreds of foam pressed into a continuous sheet eight feet across. Most of the foam pieces were pink or yellow.

Nan pushed the carpet back as she worked, until a section was free. She rolled it loosely and dragged it to the back door, heaved it off the deck onto the lawn. In that short drop it unfolded into a neat ensign, half brown jute, half sculptured champagne polyester.

The padding followed, floating out and settling its Easter-basket colors over the carpet and the uncut grass, very green in the long light of early morning.

The floor now was nothing but underlayment, splintery plywood stamped with the names of lumber companies or blurry symbols, trees and triangles, in the colors of ink that are pressed into government-inspected hams. And pencil-marks, numbers, doodles, good intentions.

Dave had left his radio. She played it very loud, stomping on the underlayment, the hollow basement booming, the bare rooms echoing. She danced with her feet apart and her arms waving above her head. Her body was levers and pulleys, muscles working against bone, and she felt a warm sweetness as she whirled and kicked.

That night, she slept on the bare floor in the bedroom, the comforter rolled around her like a sleeping bag. The house was open to the warm breezes, again, little brown bats navigating through the skeleton, the stars moving across the spaces where windows had been.

* * *

The Saturday work party arrived with galvanized tubs, ice, cases of beer and soda. Angelo and Dave and Rick had brought their friends, neighbors, wives and kids. Someone's mutt lollopped back and forth, barking.

All that stood anymore at 16 Morris Lane was the framing under a roof stripped of its shingles and plywood. The low hills beyond, the other houses on their acre lots, were sectioned by the 2-by-4s and the isosceles triangles of the trusses.

A limber boy, his chest still smooth, shinnied up one corner to attach a chain to the trusses.

Nan started up the other side. She clenched the wood with her sneakers and knees, slowly working her way to the angle of wall and roof, clinging there while she pulled up the heavy chain with the cord she'd tied to her waist.

She looked past the corner to the trees, into the neighboring garden where people bent, unconcerned, over their plantings, and far away to the river glinting as it bent west. She looped the chain around the truss and fastened it with the clamp. The boy half slid, half leaped from his corner, but she paused, aware of the ten feet to the ground, that a mistake would mean a broken ankle, a splintered collarbone. She crabbed to the railing, then leaped from there to the ground.

Two trucks rolled carefully away from the house, until the chains went equally taut at their trailer hitches. Then, with a starter's signal from Dave, they gunned forward, tires spinning, and the trusses creaked, cracked, fell, bringing the shell down with them, the whole thing slumping into the cellar hole.

The squares and angles were broken. The violence of nails and screws was ended. Words that had welded the whole thing together went back into the air, into the syrup-colored light. As the dog barked and the crowd cheered, dust rose in thinning clouds, like newly hatched gnats flying upward on the warm air.

Stranger Now

Vivian Hague Satterwhite

My heart falls when I look up from my coloring book and see Mama putting on makeup. She never does that 'less we're going to church or she's going out. It's way after dark on Saturday night, so I know it ain't church. "Mama," I whine, "you going to Jeejay's?"

"Ummhmm." She draws a black line on each eyebrow.

"Aunt Pinky going, too?"

"Yes."

"I have to go to Miss Verdie's again?" I pout.

"You know you always do, baby." She reaches for a heart-shaped compact.

I jump up and throw my coloring book against the wall. "I don't like it there! She's ugly, her clothes are ugly, her house is ugly!"

"Now don't be bad, Shara," Mama scolds, brushing burgundy blush across her cheeks. "Miss Verdie is a nice woman."

I stomp across the room and fall on the bed, kicking my skinny legs in the air and crying, watching Mama through hot tears.

She picks her short black hair into a curly scramble, hangs African earrings on her ears, and rubs "Mellow Mauve" lipstick on her lips. She puts on her new blue dress, and I'm yelling louder and kicking harder.

She turns from side to side in front of the mirror, not even noticing me. By the time she steps into high heels and sprays cologne in whispery squirts along her arms, I am tired, the bed is a rumpled mess, and Mama is sleek and beautiful.

Aunt Pinky rushes in without knocking, all breathless and pretty in a shiny gold jumpsuit, her long braids swinging and bright with golden beads. "You ready, girl?" she asks Mama. "I wanna have a good time tonight!"

She sees me sad on the messy bed, frowns, and starts talking hateful: "You let this spoiled brat tear up your bed like that?"

Mama picks up her new sequined purse. She never gets mad or upset about anything.

"I'd bust her butt!" Aunt Pinky grumbles.

"You're not my aunt," I mumble real low. It's true. She's not even one itsy bit of kin to me. She's just my mama's friend.

Aunt Pinky gives me a mean look, and puts her hands on her hips. "What did you say, girl?" She's always calling everybody "girl".

Mama heads toward the door. "Okay, you two; let's go." Her purse is winking white-silver-blue in the light.

*　*　*

Miss Verdie's in her chair, in her old faded robe, listening to the Carolinas' Christian Voice station.

I'm sunk in the corner of the saggy sofa, my breath coming in quivery shudders, missing Mama.

Miss Verdie looks over at me with her slow droopy eyes. "Everything's gonna be all right, honey. She'll be back soon."

My breath catches on a leftover cry, and I sink deeper into

the sofa's brown hollow. What kills me about this house is that everything seems to be some sick shade of brown. Even the light through the lampshade has a muddy glow that doesn't reach the corners of the room, where shadows hide behind shadows. I want to get up outa here and go racing home, but it wouldn't be the same without Mama.

On the radio, someone's singing the Lord's Prayer; the clear words cruising the air like birds on crystal wings. I'm getting sleepy, and I see Miss Verdie's already gone; her chin touching her chest, her arms folded across her stomach.

Everything my mama eats goes straight to her hips, she says. I guess everything Miss Verdie eats goes to her arms. They look too heavy for her short body, and blobs of fat hang from the elbows. They make me think of chocolate hams.

The Lord's Prayer rises on faster wings, eases down and goes away. The clock cuckoos from the mantel...I feel myself sliding into a weak, sad sleep...

I wake up quick—my heart beating so hard it sounds like it's thumping outside me. I see Miss Verdie's head snap up. She stares at the door.

I realize the sound is not my heart, but someone knocking loud.

"Who is it?" Miss Verdie calls.

"Me!" a deep voice answers. "Open up! Come on, let me in!"

"Lord!" Miss Verdie turns the radio off and struggles up, the arthritis in her knees making little dry clicks. "I'm coming!" Her voice is high and different now. She's walking kind of stiff, but trying to hurry.

I turn and peep over the back of the sofa.

She opens the door, and a bony guy that I don't know steps in fast—shoving the door closed with his foot. "Hey," he says, "let me hold a few bills!"

Miss Verdie looks him up and down. "John!"—saying the

name like she's hurting. "What in the world have you done to yourself?"

He rubs his hands together. "Ain't got time for no jaw-jackin'. Come on, I need some cash!" His eyes are swollen and shadowy.

Miss Verdie starts talking low and trembly: "You show up after all these years — and the first thing you do is ask for money!"

The guy's making little hyper moves, like he's trying to scratch, but can't find the itch. His chapped lips shape into a grin, but his eyes don't look like they laughing. "Cut the crap," he says.

Miss Verdie just keeps on staring. "You sure do look awful." Her voice is soft-sad, like she's 'bout to cry. "You've lost so much weight!"

He moves toward her, frowning. "Look, woman, get me some money now!"

"My Lord! You are on that ol' stuff, just like they said you was."

He's breathing faster. "Don't make me do this."

Miss Verdie shakes her head a little. "You're a stranger to me now," she tells him in that soft-sad way; "like somebody I don't even know."

"Please — don't — make — me — do this!" He sounds like he's praying. He reaches inside his jacket — and the next thing I know, a pistol's pointing at Miss Verdie.

Everything seems to slow down, like when I'm dreaming 'bout trying to get ready for the school bus, but can never get ready. I hear a scream, but don't know it's from me 'til I see the guy look my way for the first time, his eyes crazy with surprise.

His arm swings to aim at my head, the gun gleaming terrible in the muddy light.

I'm froze in place as Miss Verdie takes a side step between us, like she's waltzing without a partner, and the shot booms out in the room. Miss Verdie falls, blood running out all over her shoulder.

Blood…and the clock ticking quick across the quiet. "Take the money," Miss Verdie says, her voice tired. "Bedroom…top drawer…the chest."

The guy runs to the bedroom and flips the light switch. The old dark brown chest with claw-monster feet is straight ahead.

With his gun-free hand, the guy fumbles around in the drawer, then starts throwing things out. Fluffy, bright, pretty things that flow down and drop in soundless folds all over the floor: silky scarves, flowery handkerchiefs, squares of fancy lace! When he finds the crumple of money, he rushes out of the room — stepping on fuchsia, magenta, lime. It's like the colors of my crayons have bloomed across the floor.

He stops beside Miss Verdie, who's moaning pitiful. He stands there looking down at her, and the crazy seems to leave him for a moment. "I'm sorry, Mom," he says — and runs out into the night.

I make myself move, to go to the phone and dial 911.

* * *

The sirens screaming across town attract a crowd. Before I know it, the porch is packed with people: neighbors, and customers from Jeejay's.

In the living room, paramedics are working on Miss Verdie, and policemen are snooping around. Mama's holding me tight and crying.

"He tried to shoot me, Mama."

"Oh, my god! Are you all right, baby? Are you okay, sweetie? Are you?"

"Yes, Mama. For real." I feel like I'm in a movie!

Aunt Pinky isn't saying anything; just standing there with her hand over her mouth, like she's scared. I guess all this really messed up her good time.

"Who shot you, ma'am?" a policeman asks Miss Verdie.

She looks at me—then up at the cop. "I didn't know him," she says quietly. "He was a stranger to me."

*　*　*

It's Saturday night again, and Mama's putting on makeup. But my heart don't fall, 'cause Miss Verdie's home from the hospital and we're going to visit her.

Everybody knows now it was her son that did it, but I didn't tell—honest. The other day, I heard Aunt Pinky tell Mama that he bought crack with the money, and had stole that gun from someone else. He's in jail now, and I hope he stays for ever and ever!

I close my coloring book and pick up the bright yellow rose from the nightstand. "Are you ready, Mama?"

"Ummhmm." She sprays cologne in whispery squirts; takes me by the hand.

*　*　*

Miss Verdie's in her chair, listening to the radio. She turns the volume down, so that the hymns are below the words that she and my mama say: "I'll never be able to thank you enough for risking your life for Shara."

Miss Verdie looks down at her hands, like she's sort of embarrassed. "Shara's same as a granddaughter to me."

Mama hugs her and kisses her on the forehead.

I step forward, holding up the rose, feeling shy. "For you," I whisper.

Miss Verdie smiles, and her eyes look happy. "Why, how precious!" she says, touching the petals lightly with her fingertips. She looks at me kinda like she's sorry 'bout something. "I wish I had something to give you, honey, but I don't have anything that a little girl would like."

"You gave Shara all that you could when you stepped in front of that bullet!" Mama says.

Through the open bedroom door, I see the old chest, full of secret beauty. "But you do," I tell Miss Verdie.

"Well, what, honey?"

"Something from there." I point.

"Shara!" Mama's using her scolding voice.

Miss Verdie stands up.

"Well, just come on in here and show me."

I'm not tall enough to see inside the top drawer, so I stand on a footstool. In the jumble of colors, there's something that looks like little pieces of light. I reach in and pull out a purple scarf, thin as smoke, with silvery glitter woven through it. "This," I say, "oh, this!"

"No!" Mama sounds mad.

Miss Verdie pats my cheek. "It's yours, sugar. Now let me get a vase for this lovely flower." She and Mama go into the kitchen.

I walk to the sofa and sink down in the corner, spreading the scarf across my lap.

They come back with the flower in a glass vase, and Miss Verdie places it on the mantel. As she settles into her chair again, smiling, I notice for the first time that she has dimples.

Mama comes to sit by me. They talk, the radio sings, the rose glows like a little moon against the brownness of the room.

I snuggle close to Mama, and rub my hand across the scarf. It feels cool-smooth, and is the color of a summer evening sky; a summer evening sky, full of stars.

Racing Home

One Bullet

Kathryn Bright Gurkin

I met her in the frozen foods department of the supermarket where I shop. She worked there as a stocker, in a thin red cotton coat. Since she didn't wear a nametag, I never knew her name; but she looked a little like Olivia Newton-John looked fifteen years ago, so I will call her Olivia. She wore no makeup and her face seemed always pinched with cold. At the height of her troubles dark smudges appeared beneath her eyes as she grew visibly thinner. Her story is, unfortunately, not a rare one.

It no longer surprises me that people tell me secrets, tell me terrible things that they have done or that have been done to them. All my life this role of confidante to nameless strangers and the indiscreet has been my portion. I listen and sometimes I learn amazing information I would never have discovered otherwise. This is her story as it came out in bits and pieces over a period of several months, among the eggs and margarine and frozen pizzas and orange juice.

Her marriage was a mess, but aren't they all? she said. She had a daughter, ten years old, a dog and then another dog to keep it company, a husband she suspected of fooling around with any number of women but especially one woman to whom her husband talked too long in the store aisles where he worked. Olivia was obsessed with this woman, followed her in her car, spied on her house and her visitors, tried to get her fingerprints on an envelope which she planned to take to the police but the envelope disappeared, then re-appeared and so on. Most of this was related at our first meeting, following my request for a certain brand of frozen broccoli. It must be something in my face,an openness of expression, or maybe I just attract nuts. I was sure I had fallen upon a full-blown case of paranoia.

But as the weeks passed and we kept meeting in the same aisle—no matter what day or time of day I shopped, there she was, restocking shelves—and more of the story emerged, the natural empathy of an older woman for a younger one outweighed my better judgment. For her part, it seemed she had rehearsed the next installment and would not let me pass until I heard it through.

Not wanting to encourage her in her monomania although she obviously needed to talk to someone, I recommended either a good lawyer or a good psychiatrist but she didn't trust that kind of help. She seemed enthralled by the drama of the situation, like a masochistic butterfly volunteering to be impaled on a collector's pin. But why?

Olivia had married someone guaranteed to break her heart, a man so well-endowed, she said, and exhibitionistic—he was a rock musician on weekends—that groupies flocked to him; but that was better, she insisted, than her first fiancée who had kidnapped her and taken her across state lines. She was underage at the time. Now she was determined that her daughter would grow up knowing what to expect of men, so that she would trust none of them. She wished, she said, that her mother would believe how miserable her husband made her; but her mother wouldn't believe her until she heard the tape recording of the husband and the other woman on the phone. That was incontrovertible evidence of his cheating. Her daughter had listened to the tape and then confronted her father with the fact that she had heard it.

Her husband—whose name I never learned—was threatening to have her "locked up" for being crazy. A neighbor called at work to say that one of the dogs was wandering beside the road, and, racing home, Olivia had to ransom it from the pound in the nick of time. Olivia made a terrible scene at the store where her husband worked, screaming insults at the other woman and following her out to her car where the man the hussy lived with waited.

By this time Olivia was photographing footprints of an unusual kind of woman's shoe found in the driveway of a place where, she was convinced, her husband and the other woman met. The footprint with its little heart motif was proof that the woman had left her car and walked over to the husband's truck. Her husband stubbornly denied everything. He was threatening divorce. She didn't want to lose her house in a divorce settlement but she earned enough to live on if worse came to worst. I have lived long enough to know that when women tell stories like this one, the urgency and the stress of living with uncertainty can make them seem hysterical and therefore unbelievable; but Olivia was becoming so desperate and so thin that I began to dread our encounters in the supermarket. "You don't know," she told me, "how much stuff goes on in supermarkets. People making out in the meat department, stealing, drug deals going down. It's scary having to stay late to close up." I believed her. She looked scared out of her wits.

I went out of town for two weeks and when I got back Olivia seemed subdued. I had never seen her so calm and quiet. She had a story to tell me, she said, so I stopped and listened.

"My girl friend and I went to that Chinese place for lunch. I always, you know, take my time choosing my fortune cookie from the plate. This time the waiter looked at me real strange while he was serving the meal. That's what I thought. There were two fortune cookies on the plate and I took one, but when I opened it, there was nothing inside." She waited. "Do you think this means I have no future?"

I assured her that fortune cookies are made by machines, that somehow one of them just didn't get the little paper strip inserted on the assembly line. "Yeah, okay," she muttered and I went on up the aisle. I was so shaken by her tone of voice that I completely forgot to buy orange juice.

I never saw her again. After three weeks I asked the manager what had happened to the young woman in frozen foods and he told me she had shot an "intruder" at her home and killed her husband. At the coroner's inquest the killing had been deemed to be in self-defense and no trial was anticipated. Her husband had come home unexpectedly from work with a virus and she had fired, she said, in terror as he came through the door.

No one where she worked seems to know where she is working now or whether she is safe and happy. I refuse to think she might have been setting me up as a potential witness in the event that she might be charged with premeditated murder. My testimony would have been hearsay evidence and inadmissible in any case, although she might not have known that, or taken it into account before she put one bullet cleanly through his heart.

Getting What You Wish For

Kathryn Etters Lovatt

The moon that night pushed off from the sky, hanging itself just behind the water tower. That close. So close and full, Benny could not stop staring at it. He stared until his eyes crossed. His eyes crossed, and the moon doubled.

From his room, by this light, he could look down on everything around him: Greystone Street in front, his bike in the drive, that hedgerow along Tilley Creek and the brace of pines beyond. With his binoculars, he could peer next door into the Willard's kitchen. There, the immortal Mr. Poo dozed in his wicker basket. In the den, Dotty, Miss Senior, stood by the picture window. She wore a nightgown the color of buttermints, cool and mouthwatering. A quarter turn, Benny estimated, to perfect focus. He was just making the final adjustments when the door flew open.

Oblivious to the binoculars and, for that matter, the moon, his mother, Priscilla, came in buttoning a fresh blouse. "Get on your shoes," she said grimly, "and come with me."

Benny recognized the tight lip of trouble when he heard it. He was up in a flash and shoving his feet into sneakers. "What's the matter?" he asked on the fly.

"Wait," said Priscilla, a finger of silence across his mouth. "I'll tell you on the way."

Step-for-step, he matched her down the stairs, through the kitchen, into the car.

"Shelton," she announced as she plowed over a patch of early-blooming azaleas, "has been shot."

This news about his favorite uncle, collector of exotic stamps and cruddy jokes, a man who loved the whole world and his mother's older sister, dumbfounded Benny. He slumped against the car door and tried to get his brain in working order.

"Don't worry," said Priscilla. "It only grazed his ear." She reached over and squeezed Benny's hand. "I expect he's ready to go home by now."

"Who would do such a thing?" Benny felt as if he'd been yanked out of a deep sleep and was still piecing together his last dream. "Who would want to hurt Uncle Shelton?"

"Nobody, honey. Nobody would. He shot himself."

Stoplight by stoplight, his mother recited a story. "An evening like any other," she began. Even as the moon followed alongside them, she had the nerve to say this.

In this version, Ina started off in the den with the big TV, Shel in the bedroom with his latest mystery. There were details about real cops-and-robbers caught on video, what the world was coming to, but Benny let that go over his head. He listened for the bang, and directly above Ina, a thud. "Anything the matter?" she called up the steps. "Honey?" she shouted. "Shelton!"

Finding him there in the middle of the floor like that, the rifle on the big hump of his belly, she doesn't guess she'll ever get over it.

"The rifle he won in the VFW raffle?" asked Benny. Shel's good luck had downright irritated Benny's father. "What a waste," he'd objected. "He'll never use it."

"It's the only gun he owns that I know of," said Priscilla lightly. "Ina says he was digging for a wooden hanger. For those nice gray trousers he had on this afternoon."

Benny fell silent trying to imagine the unimaginable: Uncle Shelton with a loaded gun in his closet, his father hanging up his own pants.

"You shouldn't even be here." Priscilla tried the radio. She went down the line, punching buttons.

"Why'd you bring me, then?" he asked testily.

"Because Ina thought it might perk Shel up. Is this radio broken?"

"Nothing will come in clear," he told her. "Nothing you'd like anyway."

"How do you know what I like?" she said with an edge he didn't recognize. She reached up and shifted the rearview mirror until she could see herself instead of the road. She tried to revive her fine hair with her fingers, checked her teeth. At last, she found her eyes, tired and dark, with shallow hatch marks at their edges. She looked away.

"What did you tell Dad?" Benny ventured.

"He was in his chair, dead to the world. I left him a note."

"A *note*?" Benny gibed, and when he heard himself, he knew he'd gone too far.

His mother turned to stone on him. "I suggest you adjust that attitude of yours, Mister." She blinked her brights and dims at the car in front the way his father might. "Speed up," she called as she honked the horn, "or get out of the way." She passed on the curve, flew over railroad tracks. The lunacy of the night was beginning to take shape.

"Sorry," he said, and was.

She reached across then and ran the back of her hand along Benny's cheek. He could smell the almonds in her hand lotion, and beneath that, the faint bite of Comet cleanser.

"You're growing up so fast," she said, but that's not how it felt to him.

He had a learner's permit, yet. He didn't understand logarithms or how to French kiss. He felt desperate and stormy. About to bust. Nights, with the lights shut off, he used to lie awake wishing for things that might change his life: drums, a mustache, the fat chance of love. But not this. Never anything like this.

* * *

It was Uncle Shel who always stepped in for whatever went missing in Benny's life. He was two grandfathers and scoutmaster. He kept Benny's picture in his wallet, gave him his desk globe, those field binoculars, a red velvet sack of foreign coins. He took him to parades, taught him to whistle and parallel park, the box step. Benny couldn't think of a single thing he'd ever done in return.

"Here we are," said Priscilla flatly. She headed for the far lot, straddled two spaces and cut the motor. Benny's mother sank her face into the cups of her hands. There, in the moonlight, the wayward ends of her hair cast a bright web around her head. "Sweet Jesus," she said, her voice trembling beneath her fingers, "I'm not up to this."

* * *

Alone in a corner of the emergency room, Aunt Ina sat wrapped in her camel coat, a pale green border of nylon pajama bottoms hanging from underneath. Black pumps, dipping to the cracks of her big toes, failed to rein in her ankles.

She stood, opening her weighty arms. With faded, smoky lips, she reached up to kiss her baby sister, then Benny. "Sweetie," she smacked. "Bless you, coming for such a silly thing." She plucked his cheeks. "Look at him, Pris, so handsome, his life in front of him." Her eyes filled up, and she pressed their rims with wadded Kleenex.

Aunt Ina patted two empty seats. "Sit," she commanded. Benny's mother took the one that put him in between. In that high voltage spot, his true purpose became clear even to him: they needed somebody in the middle, someone to make real talk impossible.

"The hospital made me call you," Ina apologized. She leaned up and over; Priscilla did the same. "They want to keep him a little while," she explained. "To make sure they didn't miss anything."

"Have they let you see him?" asked Priscilla.

Aunt Ina sat back and turned her attention toward Benny. "On a school night, too," she cooed. " Forgive me." To her sister, she said, "He's going to be a heartbreaker, all right. Just look at those teeth. Look at them Pris. Perfect!"

For Benny, there was no escape from jabber or touch or from holding assorted items as his aunt tidied her boxcar of a purse. She handed over a bale of pencils, loose mints.

"So, you have a special friend?" She passed a rain bonnet. "Your mother says they call you, these girls." She fanned the very mention of them away. "I made Shel chase me a year." Benny accepted a button inside an envelope. "I'll be." She held out an old photo in a plastic sleeve. "I didn't even know I had this—Shel with his buddies." It was typical Navy: men in uniform toasting the world.

"Where?" asked Benny, searching in vain for the barrel-chested, bald headed man he'd known his entire life.

"There," she said, pointing a short, pudgy finger. "The one with the dare-devil grin."

It was true and bewildering.

"He was always at me to see the world," Ina said. "'Be reasonable,' I told him. 'Be practical.' I thought I couldn't do without a dining set." She dished out laundry stubs and safety pins and clamps to hold her wild frizzled hair in place. She produced a clean tissue from her pocket.

Out of the corner of his eye, Benny saw how chicken-skinned his mother looked under those lights, as if she were cold and trying to hold down supper.

"We all feel badly," she apologized, glancing his way. Both of them had been yawning through Shel's tales of glory lately. Just that afternoon, Ina had caught them drifting.

"Goodness alive, Shelton," she'd chided, all the while gathering herself and her plate up for another go at the Holiday Inn buffet. "You're putting us to sleep with those old yarns of yours." Shel grew red, and Ina said to the table, "He's been down in the dumps lately, too. Don't deny it. 'What else could you want?' I ask him. 'Look at your business. Look at this beautiful house. A Cadillac,' I say, 'Shelton, did you ever in your wildest dreams imagine that?' He gives me the silent treatment. You know why? Because he has everything. Everything." She took a noisy slurp of her tea. To Shelton, she said, "Eat! Eat and forget what's over and done with. What difference does any of it make now?"

Stripped down and bloodless, Shelton had looked a miserable sight. Even Benny's father noticed; it moved him enough to make a stab in Shel's defense.

"Let him be," he said. "He's entitled."

"He could talk about something besides the past," Ina argued. "You'd think he'd spent his life sailing the seven seas."

"Close your ears if you don't want to listen," Benny's father retorted. "Hell, I haven't heard a word a one of you've said in years."

"That's for sure," Benny's mother piped in. She was keen to brighten things up, but it was way too late for that.

Uncle Shelton made no reply, but the spoon shook as he stirred his coffee.

When it was time to go, he and Ina forked off outside the restaurant. They went to their car; Benny's family got in theirs.

"Gosh," whispered Priscilla. "My lunch is stuck in my throat."

"Everywhere you turn these days," said Benny's father, "baked potatoes."

Ina rolled down her window. "Toodle-loo," she yodeled.

* * *

But Benny felt sorry for his aunt now. She kept coming to attention as doctors swung through.

"They treat the worst first," Ina told them. "That's only fair."

And so they waited.

The three of them watched what came and went: fevers, sprains, people with sudden, sharp pains. Some of them brought friends or relatives, who, in turn, brought boxes of extra crispy and babies wanting sleep.

At the end of the second hour, Priscilla said, "Ina, you want me to talk to the receptionist?"

"Don't waste your time," Ina insisted. "They never know anything."

"We can remind them we're out here. That we're worried about what's taking so long."

"I knew I shouldn't bother you," sniffed Ina and silenced her sister once and for all on the subject of waiting.

The three of them sat like stones under the evening news, talking in spurts, running out of steam. They listened as the Coke machine on the far wall swallowed coins, listened to cups dropping, sometimes not dropping, the spray of drink in the cup or down the drain, sprinkles of ice. Each sound — their words or the words of others, the scrapes and squeaks of moving about — bounced against marble floors, bounced back.

And then Ina's tongue loosened. She talked about the cost of things and what they were really worth, how bad her night vision was getting. She recalled the summers before she married, how lean love kept her. "A waist a real man could wrap his hands around," she said dreamily. She grieved over Grandma's pearl ring again, the way it disappeared the very day she died, which made Ina think of Percy, her darling cat, disappearing, and that made her think of her sweet babies, the ones she couldn't have.

And hey, she used to dance, did Benny know that? "But it was your mama who could do the hula."

"The hula?" Benny said. "Really?"

"Grass skirt." Ina crossed her heart. "Halter top. The whole bit."

"Please," said Priscilla, flushed, but, oh, she was smiling.

His mother, dancing. Benny couldn't get over it, and under the flicker of a long fluorescent tube, he wrestled with the idea of her life before him, outside of him, a secret life. By the time the light sank to a throb, which wasn't very long, he was back thinking of himself, of tomorrow, a day off, a Monday no less, and he noticed the room had dwindled down to only them and a man with a hardback book.

Still, they asked no questions, but sat tight, holding to the chance now that nothing had actually happened, that Shel would pass through those doors any minute now, laughing. Any minute. And then they could all leave this place together, leave happily, and go back home, back to how things were.

But Shelton didn't come, and in the black coffee hours of real night, the two women began to doze. Their heads fell against Benny's shoulders, but he kept awake. Why, he wondered, and why today? Except for the moon, what was any different? Well, better to shoot yourself for the sake of a moon than a Sunday brunch.

Eventually Benny came around to the better question: Why not? It was as good a day as any: small and easy to lose, counting for nothing, at least not enough, adding up anyway.

The doctor stood at the door, waving. Benny poked his mother and Aunt Ina awake. The doctor motioned Ina to him. He gestured Priscilla to come along. Benny clutched Aunt Ina's elbow and began guiding her forward. .

Priscilla stepped in his path. "Where do you think you're going?"

"Never mind," Ina said softly. "He's a big boy now."

Priscilla fell back, and the three of them moved together.

"The wound is not a worry," the doctor said. "He's in no danger from that." Ina narrowed her eyes to read the fine print. "He's had a lot of excitement. A lot of people asking questions. Difficult questions." The doctor seemed to want to stop there, but he could tell it wasn't going to be enough. "He's resting now. He needs to rest. You should go home and rest yourself."

Ina drew herself up, slung her shoulders into her short back, a cat ready to fight. "I'm staying," she declared.

The doctor shrugged, not an all-right, not an of-course. It was a no-skin-off-my-back kind of shrug. He swept his arm around the room they stood in. "Make yourself comfortable then," he snapped. "There's no fourth floor waiting room."

Benny looked away from all of them, looked to the green concrete wall. So there it was, the absolute truth. Fourth floor was the nut ward, everybody in town knew that. You could see the windows from the elementary school; from the playground, you could see the steel bars across them.

Fourth floor was the place some people liked to tell other people they belonged. It was where kids were driving teachers and parents and it was where they put you if you tried to kill yourself. The law in this state required it.

Ina made no move, just stood there, pressing both hands against her diaphragm. Priscilla, confounded beside her, looked like a sleepwalker. Benny made himself as small as possible.

Their pitiful spectacle must have thawed the doctor.

"I'm sorry," he said. "But I'm exhausted." He put his hand on Ina's shoulder. "You look exhausted, too," he said gently. "What good can come of that?"

"Here I am," she said defiantly. "And here I'll stay. When Shelton is in his right mind again, I want him to know that."

The doctor nodded. "All right, then," he yielded. "All right. Come with me. We'll give you a bowl of tomato soup, and I'll call upstairs. We'll see if they can't pull a couple of chairs by the nurse's station."

"Tomato soup," Ina whimpered. "I'd like that."

Benny and his mother watched Ina disappear behind double doors.

"Okay," Priscilla said with relief. "Okay."

* * *

Outside, that old moon again. Ghastly blue and translucent now, it stood distinctly off-center, already on the down slope, and yet it still produced a powerful light. Its glow poured across signs and shrubs and polished the chrome on cars.

Priscilla flicked her head heavenward. "A moon like that," she said, "could make anybody crazy."

"You think he's crazy?" Benny asked. "You think that's it?"

"No," she said. She pulled up his arm and draped it around her shoulder, put her arm around his waist.

They walked entwined like that, past pole lights and a row of dogwoods trying to flower. A breeze fluttered by, shivering the trees along the concrete walk, but in this bright night, even shadows looked rooted and conspicuous, as if, just this once, they had nothing to hide.

When they came to their parking place, Priscilla reached in her pocket and fished out the car keys. "Don't slouch, " she said, putting the keys in Benny's hand and folding his fingers around them.

"All by myself?"

"Yep. But don't let me hear about how you went racing home. Take it easy."

Benny put his hands in his pockets and looked at his shoes. "I knew it," he blurted out. "I knew it all along."

"Hmm," she conceded. "There aren't many secrets on a night like this."

"Tell me one then," Benny asked gamely. "Tell me a secret."

She gave him a weary smile. "All right," she slowly agreed. "Which news do you want first?"

"The bad news." He always took the bad news first.

His mother leaned against the car, looking beyond the great beyond, the night written all across her face.

"Nothing lasts," she told him, her voice brimming with apology.

"Nothing lasts?" He stalled, committing the image of her at that moment, pale and groggy, full of secrets she would never tell, to memory. "Okay," he said. "So is that your good news, too — nothing lasts?"

She kissed her finger and reached over and put the kiss on Benny's ear. "That's my boy," she said and turned to go.

"Hey!" he said before she got too far. "That's not much of a secret."

She turned again, turned and smiled, but all the while, she went on walking, walking slow and backwards, moving further away.

Been To Baltimore

Ed Devany

"Sweet Jesus, Tyrone, get outa the mens' way so th ey can do they job!"

"I ain't botherin' 'em, granny, I swear I ain't."

But he was. He couldn't help it. Six weeks of being kept in, constantly told, *Be quiet! Walk on tiptoe. Stop 'at singing, you know yo' daddy's sick,* had just about done in the five-year-old. Now the sight of the bald-headed man on the ladder passing folding chairs through the window to his two assistants inside signaled some-thing exciting was finally about to happen. A party? Well, not the way they were lining the chairs up in church-meeting rows in the living room. Church meeting? He hoped not. He had endured enough praying the past six weeks to last him a hundred and sixty years, at least.

"What's these chairs for—some kind of party?" he asked one of the assistants, a fuzzyheaded little man who reminded him of one of the gingerbread men granny baked every Chris tmas.

"Ssshhh!" the fuzzyhead hissed like a radiator.

"Hey, peanut," the bald-headed man beckoned from the window. Tyrone ran to him hopefully. "Yessuh?"

"You want to make you fifty cents?"

"Yessuh!"

"Ask yo' granny can you come down and help pass chairs up from the hearse."

"What's the hearse?"

"The black kind of truck looking thing out front."

* * *

"Granny, man wants to know can I help pass chairs up from the hearse."

Granny's eyes got all watery, the way they'd been doing two or three times a day since his daddy got sick. "Don't you know what them chairs is for, Tyrone?"

"He said he'd pay me fifty cents."

Now the water overflowed her eyelids, running down her cheeks. "Lord'a mercy, Tyrone, you...Oh, all right, but you tiptoe past yo' daddy's room, you hear me?"

But Tyrone ran, clumping down the stairs 'like a herd of cows through a hole in a fence' granny'd called it once, getting outside in the sun at last, free.

The hearse was black as licorice, inside and out, with some kind of silver track running along the center of the floor, chairs stacked on either side of it. Tyrone tried to take two at a time, but one was all he could manage. Still, the bald-headed man was grateful.

"You saving my life, peanut, my corns was killing me, doing all the toting by myself."

"What's these chairs for?"

"Yo' granny ain't tole you?"

"No suh."

"Well, you ask her later. Ain't my place to be saying what's hers to say."

The bald-headed man ended up giving Tyrone a dollar, "Not as pretty as a fifty cent piece, but worth twice as much."

Tyrone was trying to see how many times he could fold it over when the woman in red with the fox fur piece came sauntering along.

"Man, look at them shakers wiggle," the bald-headed man whistled.

"What's *shakers?*"

"Boy, you got yo' dollar, now go on back in the house."

Tyrone started to protest when he saw granny at the window wearing her 'I've had it with you, boy' look and gesturing fiercely to 'get on up the stairs this minute,' then she disappeared back into the darkness.

In no hurry to return there, Tyrone took his time, especially after he saw the woman in red walk up to the bald-headed man. She sure looked like something special, like she was painted on the side of the ice cream truck, a bright red snow cone or popsicle you could see from three blocks away.

Suddenly his arm was yanked almost out of its socket.

"Git up them stairs this minute, you hear me?!" Granny cracking him like a whip, sending him racing home for the apartment stoop.

He scurried into the hallway, intent on going upstairs when granny's voice stopped him.

"Go on 'way from here, Hoe!"

Tyrone slipped the screen door shut with his foot, then pressed up against it to see what was going on—granny was bearing down on the woman in red.

"He called me, Momma Morgan, told me he was…"

"Don't say it!" granny cut her off. "Go on back to Baltimore. You broke his heart once. Ain't gonna have you doin' it again."

"He ain't passed yet?"

"No, he ain't, so don't you come down here trying to speed things up."

"Then how come the hearse already here? Looks like *you* the one speeding things up."

"Doctor say he ain't gonna make it through the night, and they was six other families out to rent them chairs, so…ain't none of yo' business. Go on 'way from here."

"He asked me to come, to see him, and Tyrone."

"Oh, no! Oh, no you ain't. You been to *Baltimore*, done everything they is to do against God and against nature. Tyrone don't even know who you *is*, so go on. Git!"

"I been on a bus all night long, Momma Morgan, and ain't about to turn back without seeing my mens."

"Yo' *mens*?! You been to *Baltimore* with yo' *mens*—God only knows how many of 'em, so don't come back here calling the two you left behind yo' *mens*," which was when Tyrone pushed so hard against the rotting screen his head came right through it. Granny scooted over to him like a fighting rooster.

"I told you get upstairs, Tyrone. Now go, before I tan yo' hide so hard you'll think you're seeing Jesus riding into Jerusalem. Git!"

Tyrone ran up the stairs, granny after him, huffing and puffing like an asthmatic Big Bad Wolf. The woman in red came after her and, when Tyrone glanced back as he opened the door to their apartment, he saw granny swinging her hips wildly from wall to wall to keep the woman from slipping past.

"Go in and lock the door, Tyrone!" she gasped, losing her footing and slipping, leaving a gap through which the woman in red bolted like a rat.

"Lock the door, Tyrone!"

But Tyrone ran in instead, straight into his father's room to the great bed where his father was trying to prop himself up on his elbows.

A moment later, the woman in red came in, fox fur askew, hat dangling from one bobby pin still holding it to her hair.

"Candy?" his father whispered weakly.

Then granny came charging in. Seeing she was too late, she stood panting, trying to suck in air enough for whatever disaster she was certain would follow.

The woman in red moved quickly to his father and took him into her arms, weaving about and keening over the frail body.

"Marcus, Marcus, dear God, I'm sorry."

His father's voice was fading down to a rattling whisper, out of which came words, "It's alright... Come here, Tyrone. This here's yo' momma." Then, "She's been to Baltimore," almost a gurgling, punctuated with screams from both women as his arms fell limp.

*   *   *

Curled up in the lap of the still sobbing woman, Tyrone had dozed off when a sound like a bee zooming close to his ear startled him awake.

"What's that?"

"Just zipping up the..." When he tried to turn his head toward the source, "Don't look just yet."

Tyrone heard two men hefting a heavy sack and lugging it out of the room and down the hall. Then the woman loosened the grip she had on his head. He turned to see his father's bed, empty.

"Where daddy?" he inquired of her reddened eyes glistening with tears.

"He gone to his reward," she whispered.

"In Baltimore?" Tyrone asked her.

Durango

Kim Church

On the bus to Colorado she let him touch her. His fingers were familiar as an odor; the nails scraped and made her cringe. "Hurry," she whispered, "before somebody sees." But it took forever, it always did, with her thinking the whole time, *Stop, No more*, gripping the armrest until her hand throbbed and her fingers swelled. "Please," she said out loud. The urgency in her voice was not pleasure. This was not pleasure.

Finally he withdrew and she let go. Lifted her hand off the sticky vinyl and shook it dry, trying not to think of her own sweat mingled with the dirty sweat of strangers, trying not to think at all. She slumped against the window and stared out at New Mexico, an endless brown shining hot nothing.

"Hey, look." He pointed across her, his arm grazing her throat. "Antelopes, a whole herd." Outside the window one layer of brown shifted sideways. The fleeing herd looked like a wave of brown heat, warped and surreal. "Do you want the binoculars?" he asked, but she didn't look away from the window. She was remembering El Paso, the fumes of heat rising off the sidewalk when they'd gone down this morning to buy tickets, and the man outside the Trailways station, how he'd come at them, clumping forward in his square-toed boots until he was standing so close she could barely breathe. He had a brutal smell, salty and sour. "Got a dollar?" he'd asked her, and she held her breath, actually thinking to herself: I'm going to die. But before anything could happen, her husband fished a few coins out of his pants pocket and pressed them into the man's grimy hand, then turned to her just like that and asked her did she want new boots for her birthday because the Tony Lama discount store was only a block away.

Just like that.

He had a knack, her husband, for figuring out even before she did exactly when she'd reached her limit—something he'd learned after years of marriage, years of testing, to calculate with near-mathematical certainty. She wasn't sure how he could know. Maybe something in her face gave her away. Maybe this morning it had been the heat itself that warned him, that choking dusty sunlight, who could say. But he always sensed when to relent, when to give her an opening. Now he'd done it again, this time with birthday boots.

She crossed her legs and flexed the gray python-belly uppers, pointed the sharp toes. She had picked them out herself and they were absolutely beautiful. So beautiful she had to let him touch her.

*　*　*

They are spending her birthday with Mary and Tye in Durango. After a late dinner they unfold the webbed lounge chairs in the field beside the house, settle back under blankets, drink blue margaritas out of tumblers and wait for the meteor shower.

"Cygnus," her husband is saying, "the swan." He knows the name for everything. He raises his tumbler and draws a cross against the sky. "That one, his tail, is Deneb. That's his head halfway between Vega and Altair. I should've brought out the binoculars. You can see how his neck stretches down the Milky Way. And that dark stripe along his side, like a valley? That's where the galaxy divides."

The others are quiet. She jiggles the ice in her glass impatiently. Kicks off her boots, tucks her feet under her blanket. The August night is chilly, even for Durango. The stars seem frozen in place.

"I haven't seen the first meteor," she says. "Nothing's moving."

"Not exactly true," her husband says. "It only looks like nothing's moving because we're so far away."

"I could make another pitcher of margaritas," Mary offers, without getting out of her lounge chair. Pale hands folded serenely across her blanket, Mary is the picture of everlastingness.

"I don't get it," Tye says. "Usually we'd be seeing them by now. Two nights ago we would've seen thirty by now."

Her husband says, "That's how they figured out the universe was infinite, you know. The absence of parallax."

"Sounds like a movie," Tye says.

"No matter how much you move around, the stars don't. They don't appear to move in relation to ea—"

"There!" she shrieks. "There goes one!" A miracle—their first shooting star, and she's the first to see it. And on her birthday, no less. She's breathless, they all are, watching as the breakaway star arcs across the sky, racing home. Even after it drops behind the ridge she keeps her face pressed to the sky, expectant. The cold night air feels like a windowpane, a glassy barrier so brittle it could shatter—it could, she thinks. The air could shatter. She could shatter it. She has only to stand up and a thousand icy slivers will fall away and leave nothing between her and the meteors.

Next to her, her husband is talking again. Maybe he understands the physics of what's happening, maybe he knows the name for this instant in which everything impossible becomes possible. She's not listening. She's peeling off her blanket, rising, giddy with purpose, weightless as starlight.

Fish Camp

Joseph Bathanti

After turning off the main road, they passed between two gravel silos, bumped over the railroad tracks, then followed a dirt road that finally emptied into the restaurant's parking lot. It was crowded with cars and a loose assembly of dogs pacing about it.

"Perfect directions," the man driving said to his wife.

"Why in the world is it way back here?"

"I guess because of the lake. It's called Dream Lake Fish Camp."

The restaurant sat on stilts in the middle of a murky pond.

"And why do they call it a fish camp?"

"You know, I don't know. We'll have to ask."

"It's crowded, judging by the cars. That's a good sign."

The man got out of the car, opened one of the doors and unharnessed the sleeping baby from his car seat. He noticed above the restaurant, on the jagged pine horizon on the far shore, a sudden flash like heat lightning—no sound. There were two more as he stood there gathering the baby and his various livery. He started to say something about it to his wife, but she'd obviously not seen it. She was looking in the mirror on the underside of the passenger's sun visor and brushing her close-cut hair which was much shorter than her husband's which hung to his shoulders.

"Ann," he said. "How do you feel about this whole thing?"

"Eating here?"

"No. Our coming to live here. The move. Accepting the position."

"I'm thrilled, Arthur." She put her hand on his. "I really am. It'll be wonderful. This is all we've talked about for so long. I don't think I could take another year in the city."

"Really?"

"Yes. Absolutely."

The minute she got out of the car two of the dogs sidled over, then fell quivering at her feet when she spoke to them. They were skeletal and their coats were patched with mange. At the approach of the dogs, Arthur had walked around to her.

"Look at these poor creatures," she said. "They're starving." She looked about at the other dogs limping among the parked cars or simply propped on their legs staring at her. "They're all starving."

"C'mon," said Arthur, taking her arm and urging her toward the restaurant.

"Look at them."

"I know, Ann. But I'm not sure what we can do about it."

"Why doesn't someone feed them? Who do they belong to?"

"Honey, I don't know the answers to these questions."

"For God's sake, Arthur."

There was another flash. "Did you see that?" asked Arthur.

"What?"

"Nothing."

The dogs yowled at the flash. The baby opened his eyes, popped his head from his father's shoulder and said, "Dog."

His parents laughed. He then said, "God," and they laughed even more. These had been his first two words, were in fact his only two words, and he used them interchangeably at the sight of dogs. Arthur tried to pat the baby back to sleep, but he was clearly awake, and the barking dogs, despite Arthur's attempts to shoo them away, followed the family all the way to the door of the fish camp.

The place was much larger than it looked from the outside. It was jammed with long folding tables, each arrayed with a complement of squeeze bottles, plastic lemons and an ashtray. The walls had painted onto them portholes and various scenes of nautical life, and tacked up at intervals were trophy fish: large-mouth bass, bluegills, a marlin, a swordfish and a few pike. The restrooms were labeled "buoys" and "gulls." Just inside the door, a small dark man dressed in the white uniform of a cook stood ringing up tickets at a cash register. Next to it were a jar of mints and a placard with the staring faces of missing children. As the man punched the register keys, he shifted a toothpick from one side of his mouth to another. Pinned to his shirt was a little button with his name, "Fulton," and in the waistband of his trousers, the duct-taped butt of a small pistol bulged.

As Arthur and Ann stood there wondering what to do, the hostess, dressed in a sailor blouse and white slacks, as were the waitresses, handed Ann two menus and said, "Sit anywhere."

"We'd like the non-smoking section," said Ann.

"Honey, it's all the same," said the hostess over her shoulder as she walked away.

When they walked into the restaurant proper, it were as though they had mounted a proscenium and the lights had come up on them. It seemed each face interrupted its business to stare. Ann smiled, but Arthur fell into his tick of mumbling unconsciously to himself, a defense he had developed over the years whenever he felt uncomfortable. Ann could hear him: "Do we know these people? Who are these people? What the hell are they looking at?"

She linked her arm through his. "Arthur," she said. They chose a table by a window and eventually the faces returned to their plates.

"Well," said Arthur as if recollecting himself. He opened a menu. The baby had fallen back to sleep on his shoulder. A flash to his left through the window. He turned to it. Then two more.

"What in the world?" said Ann.

"I know," said Arthur. "I saw them earlier, but I didn't want to say anything."

"Why?"

"I don't know."

"What do you suppose they are? Heat lightning?"

"I guess."

"It's the movie," said their waitress who pranced up and put a bowl of hushpuppies in front of them. "The castle's under siege. They're making a horror movie over to the old rock quarry and the flashes are special effects. Look, there's another."

Another flash spread over them, then the vague sound of dogs.

"Drives them dogs crazy," said the waitress.

"Who do the dogs belong to?" asked Ann.

"Don't know. Somebody should put 'em out o' their misery."

"They're starving."

"Precisely my point," said the waitress. "My name's Cindy. Do y'all know what you're gonna have?"

Ann had picked up and bitten into one of the hushpuppies. "These are good. What are they?"

"Hushpuppies."

"Mmm. Have one, Arthur."

Arthur didn't seem to hear. He was studying the menu.

Flashes came in a burst.

"You never had hushpuppies?"

"No," replied Ann. "What's in them?"

"Corn meal batter, a little sugar, and onion's all. Y'all ain't from around here, are you? Y'all are with the movies, I'd guess."

"No. We're not with the movies," said Ann.

"Who's making this movie?" asked Arthur.

"A company from Wilmington. Belongs to Dino DeLaurentis, the same man who made King Kong. It's about a man finding an ancient book and once he opens it, he releases all the evils of the past and has to travel back in time to set things straight." Cindy paused and lit up a cigarette, then reached across Arthur and slid the ashtray toward her. "I'm not kidding."

"No. It's very interesting," said Ann.

Waitresses hurried by holding high trays crowded with enormous fish-shaped cardboard plates, golden food spilling from them. People ate, for the most part, silently, with a kind of grateful haste, looking up occasionally at Arthur, or so he perhaps imagined, as if he were suddenly the restaurant's one fixed point of reference.

There was one man in particular at the table closest to theirs. A very old man, sallow—yellow really—with thin red lines branching over his face like secondary routes of a road map. He wore a porkpie hat and a plaid cowboy shirt opened three buttons down, out of which spiraled a wire or tube connected to a box next to him on the floor that looked like a miniature TV. The man kept looking at Arthur, flaring his nostrils, showing his big teeth, rolling his eyes.

Across from him was an obese woman, situated more than anything, against the ladder-back chair on which she sat. Her face was a huge expressionless mask, the eyes slits, the hair cinched around her scalp as with a drawstring, the mouth at intervals yawning open to take in forkfuls of fish. Her naked arms wattled each time she lifted them.

It was near dark outside. Around the lake, at bank level, spotlights trained on the water had come on. In their glimmer the water was an impenetrable green. There was, however, on its surface a nearly imperceptible disturbance, as if tiny creatures were hurling themselves in. Arthur saw something monstrous enter the water.

"They filled the motel swimming pool with jello," said Cindy.

Ann and Arthur looked up.

"The movie people. They're big partyers. They come in here a few times, but Fulton has barred them from ever entering again. They're only allowed to come to the to-go window."

"I'd think he'd be glad for their business," said Arthur.

"They were raisin' Cain, carryin' on, wantin' t'bring beer in. I personally found it thrillin', but not Fulton. He don't monkey around."

"Fulton's the owner?" asked Arthur.

"Sure is. No nonsense. Church o'God."

"Hmm. Do you know what you want?" Arthur asked Ann.

"Yes, I think I'll have the trout. Is it fresh?"

"Ah, yeah," said Cindy. "But let me check." She set down her cigarette in the ashtray, pulled a pad and pencil out and began writing. "Fries or baked?"

"Baked, please."

"Sour cream or butter?"

"Sour cream."

"Slaw or salad?"

"Salad."

"Dressing?"

"What do you have?"

"Ranch, Thousand, Italian, French, Bleu Cheese, Oil and Vinegar."

"I'll have oil and vinegar."

"What to drink?"

"Water, please."

"Unlimited refills on the tea."

"Water will be fine, thanks."

"How about you, sir?"

"I'll have the exact same thing as my wife."

"What about for the baby?"

"I have something for him," said Ann.

"Some milk?"

"He's fine."

"Don't he drink milk?"

"He'll be fine. Thank you."

"Y'all'll need a high chair, I reckon."

"No thanks."

"He don't sit in a high chair?"

"Yes, he does. But we prefer to hold him. Thank you."

"Well, whatever."

As the waitress turned to go, Arthur said, "Miss, may we have our fish broiled, please?"

"I don't know."

"Pardon?"

"Everything comes fried."

"Well, if you wouldn't mind asking, please?"

"Alright. I'll ask Fulton. He does all the cooking."

"Thanks."

She walked off leaving her cigarette in the ashtray. When Arthur picked it up and stubbed it out, the baby opened his eyes. But he was not clearly awake. He moaned and whined and thrashed about. Arthur cooed and tried to comfort him, but the baby punched at him with his tiny fists. The old man and the fat woman got up to leave.

"Let me take him," said Ann. She took the baby, opened her blouse and began nursing him. He instantly settled down, She ran her fingers through his hair and then brushed something out of it. "Her ashes fell on his hair. There, there. Mama's little love pumpkin. Thirsty boy. Isn't he? Yes, him is."

The baby drank noisily from his mother's breast, detached himself, burped loudly, then laughed. Arthur and Ann laughed.

"Him was so hungry," said Ann.

"Dog," said the baby.

The man and woman, stalled in their departure, hovered over them. The man carried the contraption to which the wires were attached. With one hand held out, he stared at Ann's exposed breast, creeping closer, it seemed to Arthur, so that he said, more loudly than he meant, "Ann." She looked up at the man, then swiped her blouse shut.

"He's a little old for that, ain't he?" said the woman. The insides of her forearms were flaked with seborrhea.

"No, he's not." Ann managed to sound pleasant.

"How old is he? It's a boy, ain't it?" The woman fingered the toothpick in her mouth.

"Excuse me?" said Arthur

The old man stared at Arthur. His eyes were white. His nearly diaphanous teeth were locked together in a lipless grimace.

The baby hadn't taken his eyes from the old man. Perfectly composed, he sat on his mother's lap, his hands held together.

"It's alright, Arthur," said Ann. "He's just a few months past two."

"It's a mistake—lettin' him form an attachment like that," said the woman. "Cute little chap. I'll say that for'm. What's his name?"

"Doering," said Ann.

"That a boy's name?"

"It's a family name," Arthur said, giving the woman what he thought was a meaningful look.

The old man said through his teeth, "Had me a heart transplant. Got a man your age heart." Then he opened his teeth a little and hissed. A strand of bluish spittle lobbed out of his mouth and took hold on his chin. The woman took a napkin from the table dispenser, wiped it off, put it in her pocketbook, then scratched her forearm like mad.

"He's doin' just fine," she said. "Showin' no signs o' rejection."

"That's marvelous," said Ann.

"Doctors call it a miracle."

"I'm a miracle," said the old man.

"Well, I've always wanted to meet a miracle," said Arthur.

"Well, I always wanted to meet a movie star," retorted the woman.

"I beg your pardon."

"You're the movie man," said the woman. "You're on the front page near every day. I know your name. I just can't call it." She took on a pensive look and dug abstractedly at her rash.

Doering began to whine and claw at his mother's shirt.

"No, honey," said Ann.

A flash. When Arthur turned to it, he saw the thing again come out of the water. It was an alligator.

"Titus Clay," hissed the old man.

"That's it," said the woman. "You're Titus Clay."

"I'm not Titus Clay and I have nothing to do with any movie."

Just then the food arrived. Cindy set enormous platters in front of Arthur and Ann. Huge mounds of French fries, cole slaw and fried fish. Arthur and Ann looked down at the food. Doering had managed to get his hand inside Ann's shirt.

"He likes that titty is what," said the old man.

"This here's Titus Clay," the woman said.

"I knew it the minute he walked in," said Cindy. "Fulton's fit to be tied."

"I'm not Titus Clay. My name is Arthur Schoenling, not that it's anyone's business."

"We are here from Wisconsin. My husband just took a job at the college. He's a medievalist."

"Well, I don't know nothin' about that," said the woman and then abruptly walked off. The old man showed his teeth and tongue, made a retching noise and dragged himself and his console after the woman.

"God," said Doering.

"What did he say?" asked Cindy.

"Nothing," said Ann.

"He said 'God.' Didn't he?"

"Yes," said Ann.

Arthur was audibly mumbling. Ann put her foot on his and pressed.

"That is so sweet. Can I hold him?" She held out her arms to Doering. "Want to come with me? I'll take you into the kitchen and give you a cookie. C'mon."

Doering recoiled, burrowing deeper and deeper into his mother's chest, snaking his hands around inside her blouse.

"Ow," Ann said. "Doering, don't do that."

"C'mere, little precious. Give you a cookie."

"Dog," said Doering.

"Doering," said Ann, then to the waitress, "He's a little shy. If you don't mind."

"Miss, this isn't what we ordered," said Arthur. "We both asked for salads and baked potatoes and this doesn't look like trout. And we asked that it be broiled."

"I can swap the fries and slaw, but Fulton said he don't broil."

Looking at Arthur, Ann said, "No, no, leave them. They'll be fine."

"I can swap 'em."

"No. Truly. It's all fine. Thank you."

As Cindy walked off, she said, "I knew the whole time you were Titus Clay. You were good in that Nascar movie, Racing Home. That's about my favorite."

Ann yanked Doering's hand out of her blouse. "Stop it," she said. "Arthur, stop mumbling. Let's just eat and get out of here."

Doering started crying. Ann grabbed roughly at him, opened her blouse so violently a button flew, and reattached him to her breast. Arthur had begun to eat. He was still mumbling. There was an enormous flash and then the sound of yelping dogs.

"Arthur, I just saw a crocodile."

"Alligator."

"Arthur, you're eating with your hands, and please stop mumbling."

"Florida is the only place in the United States inhabited by crocodiles. What you saw was an alligator."

"Okay, Arthur, an alligator, if you want to split hairs. But a very large reptile just slid into that lake. Does that not concern you? They think you're a movie star."

"This goddamn fish has bones in it," Arthur nearly shouted.

The entire restaurant quieted and all eyes came to rest on Ann and Arthur. The only sound was Doering's loud burbling. The man they had seen earlier at the register barged through the big aluminum swing doors of the kitchen and strode straight to their table. His pistol was in his hand. He held it up to them.

"Mr. Clay, I'm obliged to ask y'all to leave."

"My name is not Clay."

"You're welcome to take your food with you. Cindy," he called, "fetch a couple of doggy bags."

Cindy, looking vindicated, sauntered over. She grabbed Ann's and Arthur's plates and started packing their food into styrofoam boxes. Ann took Doering from her breast.

"God," said the baby.

"And a kid that cusses," said Fulton.

"He does not," cried Ann.

"We're not going anywhere," said Arthur.

"I b'lieve you are." Fulton took a step closer to Arthur and leveled the gun at his chest. "Stand up Mr. Clay."

Ann was on her feet. "C'mon, Arthur. Let's leave."

Arthur stood up. "This is preposterous. My name is not Clay. I have nothing to do with any movie. I'm a medievalist."

"That's just fine, Mr. Clay. And that's your sorry business. But I don't want none of them in my restaurant neither."

Ann, with Doering and her baby bag in her arms, had already walked past Fulton toward the door. She turned. "Arthur, please?"

Arthur stood staring at Fulton. A flash so bright it illuminated the entire lake played out of the sky. Then there was an explosion and the dogs barked.

"It ain't nothin' to me to shoot you in your tracks, Mr. Clay. I've done it before in this very room."

Arthur threw some money on the table, picked up the boxes and caught up with Ann. Just as when they first entered, each eye in the place bored into them and there was the audible litany, "Titus Clay." There was a line leading into the restaurant, so they had to jostle through it to get to the parking lot. A woman in a wheelchair with a long platinum wig worked a Bell's-palsied mouth into a smile and held out to Arthur her pincer-like hand. Without even realizing what he was doing, he took it. With tremendous strength she drew him to her.

"I've seen all your movies," she whispered, and tried to kiss him. Her breath was awful. He broke away and lurched into the parking lot. Ann was screaming, holding Doering above her head. He was mouthing over and over, "Dog," as the dogs snarled and nipped at Ann. They jumped, leaving the earth completely, trying to get at the child. Arthur threw down the fish and ran kicking at the dogs. They scattered, whimpering and snarling, and quickly found the fish which they instantly devoured, styrofoam and all.

Ann was crying, holding an unperturbed Doering tightly against her. The sky above the fish camp was white with bursts like lightning breaking on the horizon, making the lake holographic.

"C'mon," said Arthur. He guided them toward the car.

"My God, Arthur," Ann said. "My God."

A low-slung smashed up Bonneville, throwing up a cloud of dust and gravel, ripped into the parking lot, fishtailing before it stopped. The driver, a terribly handsome man, got out first. His face was smeared with blood. Out of the other doors emerged three other men, dressed in medieval attire. One had a long coarse hide robe, cinched with hemp at the waist. He wore a headdress from which knifed on either side the long curving horns of a beast, and carried a long staff with what looked to be a live raven on its tip. The other two were dressed as knights. They wore plastic armor, patched in some areas with aluminum foil. Big swords hung from their belts. They smoked cigarettes through their helmet visors. The four just stared at the Schoenlings. Arthur and Ann stared back.

The driver waved. Then he lifted his other hand; and where there should have been one, attached at the forearm, was a chainsaw.

"God," said the baby.

The driver smiled and pulled the ripcord.

Death of the Smaller Parts

Kitty Lynn

On Tuesday afternoon, Margaret canceled the newspaper. She pulled on her warmest clothing: the pale blue turtleneck that the beekeeper had given her because it matched her eyes, the brown cable knit sweater from the consignment store, an undyed, raw silk neckerchief and wool socks stitched twice, a pair of leggings and a pair of jeans over that. She looked at the image in the mirror. "I don't look like myself anymore," she said to the reflection.

Margaret slipped her arm into the bloodstained dog backpack Milka had carried during those former months when they were still hiking to the beekeeper's house. Inside was a small, sealed box with a queen bee egg nestled inside. There were other eggs, too, not as large, and Margaret was counting on them to be workers and drones. The queen of this batch of eggs had always been sweet according to Bennie, and this was the sort of thing that he was capable of promising. Not much else, though.

Margaret locked the doors to her house and walked over to the doghouse in the side yard, now the marker stone for Milka's gravesite. She had buried Milka one week before and pulled the doghouse directly on top. A few days later, she painted Milka's doghouse emerald green and laid thick carpet on the plywood floor. The doghouse looked out behind her house, towards the Deep River as it wound its silvery way to Green County where Bennie the Beekeeper lived.

Now, she placed Milka's old collar around her neck. It was a perfect fit. She buckled it in on the third notch, and gave a small tug for good measure. The collar's electrical shock box pressed into her neck.

She walked to the side of the house and flipped the switch that turned on the invisible fencing. "There." She dropped to all fours. "Just like Milka."

Margaret thought back to the past week when she had tied her blue scarf around Milka as the dog lay in the small casket, and placed the doggie toys around her. With the beekeeper's help, she had dug a five-foot hole and lowered the casket into it. Every thrust of the shovel reminded Margaret of Milka's own adoration for digging holes. That's when the idea came to her and she told Bennie the Beekeeper.

"I'm going to be a dog," she had said. Bennie had laughed and kept on digging. But Margaret was determined to understand what Milka's life had been.

Margaret crawled to the doghouse, looking at the darkening sky. She felt the pitch of the earth twist, almost as if the sky was falling at a snail's pace. She was under the canopy of pines and an elm of which she heard the last autumn leaves rustling when flocks of sparrows landed lightly on its branches. The wind caressed the bodies of trees and it reminded her of the beekeeper's touch. At that time, it had been as if the whole world lay imbedded in their quiet touching. But that was before.

Before Margaret held Milka's stiff body and brushed her soft white head... *there... there...* white as river foam. Before she had released her own long moan and the wind took the moan down the narrow river channel. Before she had closed the lid forever on a death that felt like a final payment.

Margaret smelled the wild, brisk soil under her limbs and the fecund smell of the Deep River as it wafted up from the valley. She pressed her nose high. "Milka was an air sniffer," she said, and she sniffed in short, intense puffs.

*   *   *

It had been late last autumn, as she was walking the winding path along the Deep River, when she smelled something burning sweetly. Wisps of smoke drifted above her head, and she saw the beekeeper standing near his hives close to the bungalow where he lived. Smoke hung lazily in the air, rising from a piece of smoldering kindling at his feet.

Bennie moved like a swan asleep, and worked without a face net—without any protection—while bees hung happily in the air around him like little ceiling mobiles. He extracted a square tray of honeycombs clung with bees, then looked up at her where she stood peering around a big tree. She felt she knew him because she regularly enjoyed his amber honey which was sold in town, and relished its flavor of rich honeysuckle. He nodded and she sidled closer, smiling, as unconcerned as he was about the bee-filled air. His hand enclosed over hers. She noted the well-formed callous on the bottom of his hand, and his smell, which was like honey doused with burning ciders. She watched the bees that had coated his arms crawl casually onto hers.

He lowered his face, which that was decorated with a few stray bees, sleepy from the smoke. Soon, his bees became her bees, and she felt his kiss. She grew sleepy too as if he were a bee delivering honey to his queen. It was just like this that their romance had begun in the long, gray season of dying, and finally ended the following spring, like the loping away of a quarterhorse across a great, green field.

* * *

It was mid-afternoon of that first day by the doghouse, when Margaret heard screeching tires and saw Bennie's truck rounding the corner, past jessamine vines that bloomed yellow in spring, but now languished around a split-rail fence that bordered her property. She adjusted her collar, as if a strand of hair had fallen out of place. Bennie weaved on and off the road erratically; an irritating habit that often landed him in ditches and slung mud across his truck. "Bennie!" she called, and proudly walked on her knees to greet him.

He held a large, flat steaming box. He strode right through the electrical crackle of the invisible fence, then his steps became hesitant as he looked down at her. "Hellfire." He shook his head. "So you did it." Bennie stared. Honey jumped out and followed at his heels, smelling the ground along the way on a trail that led to the woods.

"Pizza!" Margaret tore into a slice, licking her fingers and inspecting his pair of white overalls and white shirt. "Remember when Milka was born on the back steps? We ate pizza that night, too. And finally I had a family!"

Bennie dipped his head. "I was never a part was I?"

"You never were," she said agreeably. "You never asked for more." Margaret wiped her mouth with a napkin, then dropped it when she remembered that a dog wouldn't do that.

Honey rushed over to sniff the napkin. Margaret leaned far over and did the same; tiny puffs of sand blew up from the ground. When she sat up, she saw Bennie shudder softly.

"We can find you another dog, Margaret," he said. She detected a hint of honey on his breath.

The pizza soured on her stomach. She turned, stood to sling the last slice away like a Frisbee towards the Canahan's house across the street. "I lost the last, smallest part that felt the closest." The slice of pizza landed on the stoop. A lot of good they were as neighbors. Didn't see a thing, Mr. Canahan had remarked, even though Milka had dragged herself bleeding across his yard.

Bennie tenderly moved a locket of hair from her eyes, and clasped her hand. He still had his firm grip, and the callous on his palm was larger.

"Find out who shut off Milka's electric fence," Margaret said. She let go of Bennie's hand and dropped to her knees, clawing furiously in the soft mulch near the tree. The dirt flew in an arc behind her. Then she leaned over and nosed the pizza box into the hole she had dug.

When she looked up Bennie and Honey were loading themselves into the truck. Honey's head and tongue were hanging out of the window. Bennie stared in silence before he started the motor and pulled away. Margaret retreated into her doghouse, stuck her head out of the opening that looked out over the river and a clear sky.

"I am part of something somewhere," she murmured.

When nightfall came, she pulled on a wool overcoat, extended the hood and zipped it up. She felt a minuscule swaying of the earth…a slight movement not strong enough to tilt her.

The stars grew brighter as the blue sky darkened, first into pale blue, then gray, and a dark charcoal until finally a fine, black star-studded coat swallowed her and she disappeared into the shadows. She counted the stars. Later, when a cold chill settled into her bones, and she gathered her limbs around herself. Everything numbered too many. She lay her head down on her tucked paws and the sweet numb feeling of sleep overtook her. She was the only one left.

* * *

Margaret awakened and lifted her head to see the opossum. He had gray paws, gray toothpick-like fur flecked with white, and long white teeth that it displayed, challenging her. She thought of the small box containing her bee eggs inside the backpack and she snarled low. The opossum backed up and waddled away towards the Deep River.

Margaret bolted like lightening from the doghouse door, sending the opossum scurrying. She lowered, neared it, her thick drool flying, her jaws wide, ready to snap, when an iron pipe slammed into her neck. She gasped, snapped onto her back, air gone from her lungs. She rolled to her side; her body shook and shuddered; her head reeled.

Then she remembered: the invisible fence. She rubbed her paw on the shock box, and curled up in a sullen ball.

The opossum's fat rustling sound wafted up. Then it whimpered like a baby. Margaret sat up, tipped her head, and after a while, her heart warmed. The wind shifted. It smelled as if the possum had entered its cubbyhole.

The sun was coming up, hidden and hazy behind the clouds. A bright light lined the horizon, like a zippered pocket slowly being opened and its treasures spilled outward. Sparrows called to each other. Little peeps and chirps came from lungs as small as the brown mole on the base of her left thumb.

Across the street, the Canahan's door swung open. Margaret smelled bacon. Mr. Canahan walked out to get the newspaper from his well-clipped yard. She wagged her tail, and gentled her expression. He winced, tucked the paper under his arm, and disappeared into the house leaving behind the smells of mint aftershave and bacon. She moaned in a rising crescendo, "Hello ...ooOOooOOOOOoooOOOOO."

When the rain came, Margaret scampered into her house. She crunched some puppy chunks. She smelled Green County in each raindrop. She stuck out her head and then her tongue, and tasted Deep River honey falling. She hummed, pleased with her new tenor voice. The rain slowed, then stopped.

Margaret lifted her head proudly out the doghouse door. She

strutted in the wet sand, displaying herself as a magnificent dog. She sniffed the morning air, proud to have run off that unattractive possum. She lapped the sweet, nutritious rainwater captured in the large bowl. Margaret retreated into her shelter, curled into a comfortable ball and fell asleep.

* * *

She heard a car door closing, and poked her head out to see a cop and a paramedic staring at her. "Yes?" she asked. After all, she hadn't lost her voice, although the shock box on the collar seemed to be heavier on her throat.

"Are you all right, Miss?" The cop asked.

"Perfectly."

"Can we get you anything?" The paramedic shifted his weight to a shoe that had a split in the lower seam.

Get me a chicken breast and biscuit. "Get off my property," she instructed.

The paramedic's face reddened. He shifted his weight again, this time to the other shoe, which displayed no defect of character. "We're here to HELP you...Miss. What are you doing living in a doghouse?"

What are you doing talking to a dog? "It's paid for," she said.

"I'm sure." He shook his head. "Anyone else living with you?"

Does it look like anyone else can fit in here? "Milka." Her heart clenched tightly. "But I buried her after I washed all the blood off her."

The police officer cleared his throat, and threw his hands up. "Certified."

"A stupid question," she pointed out. Her heart was beating madly, and she checked her hands for traces of blood.

The officer squatted, now three feet away. She smelled his aftershave. "Do you consider this normal behavior, Miss?"

"Well, of course. Otherwise, why would I be doing it?" Margaret suppressed an overwhelming urge to bite him on the leg, and slipped her head back inside the doghouse. She laid her head on the backpack, protecting the box of bee eggs.

The paramedic and officer spoke quietly, and the ground trembled. Could the planet be turning again? Why in increments? Shouldn't it be a continual rotation, pivoting around the mother sun?

Someone rapped on her doghouse, and she looked out into the officer's face.

"Miss…" the officer said, rubbing his chin.

Her mouth twisted into a faint smile.

"Miss Malorey," he began again. "Look…we've gotten a cat out of a tree, but…we've…never gotten a dog out of a… *person,* before."

"There, there," she said, distracted by his hands, which were shaped like Bennie's. Now that the urge to bite him had passed, she wanted him to scratch her head. She bent it forward for him, then heard the jangle of his handcuffs. She threw up her head, bared her teeth. "You better get out of my yard before I have to chase you out," she snarled

The cop stood and backed off next to the EMT. They smiled uneasily at each other. "This one's going to be a lot of paperwork," the cop whispered. The invisible fence crackled.

Margaret viewed every paint-peeling clapboard of her vacant house, the cop with his hat and radio and bulletproof jacket, and the telephone lines and curbs and parked cars. She smelled two kinds of antiperspirant and three kinds of pen ink and even that the cop's handcuffs and keys were made of two different metals.

"Move!" she shouted, grabbed the bloodstained backpack, pushed past the two men and began pumping her legs toward the white buzz. Closer, closer, until she closed her eyes when the long, sharp explosion coursed through her. She howled, long and hard, but kept her legs moving. Numbing exhaustion consumed her when the current finally released, but she fought it, running with mindless intention as if the lead dog of a sled team. She ran away from the invisible fence, the cop, the EMT. She ran from her house, and Bennie's house, and his boxes of hives. She ran from the prison of asphalt onto the soft earth of the forest, then flung off her shoes. They disappeared in the leaf litter. The pads of her feet hit the earth and she was racing home, unbuckling, flinging off the shock box collar, grabbing the backpack's strap between her teeth.

Inside the backpack, the small box rattled. She knew she would find a hollow tree for her queen bee.

There, Margaret thought. She sniffed the air as she sped, leaping over downed trees. Sniffed river water, moss, hardened berries and mushrooms; food enough until the bees made honey. She was the mother of Milka. *There…there.*

R a c i n g   H o m e

Sky

Heather Dune Macadam

"It's big."

"The biggest."

"I didn't think it would be."

"Me neither."

They stared out at it. Endless endlessness, stretching like cerulean cellophane tucked over a carcass of land, held up by the invisible bones of the sky. The ads were right, that's what Rebel thought, the ads were right. Another truck whipped by leaving their feet dusted with fine snow that then darkened into slush on their boot tips. She shoved her hand back under her poncho. She'd let Chyna flag the next one, when and if it came.

"We should have been there in two hours." Chyna pulled out the map and rechecked the red lipstick line she'd drawn from Salt Lake City, north. It was a fifteen-hour drive at sixty miles an hour and that's what she had planned on. Fifteen maybe sixteen hours.

They'd gone this way to add a state to their trip.

The map didn't say anything about the average length of time between pick ups per state; that would have been useful information. The map just said it was this far between here and there. Simple. Short. Just a jaunt of her finger and they were in Washington. Chyna could feel the journey going through her and see how it should happen, but it wasn't happening that way.

We'll be there in time for dinner, she'd said.

She dragged her finger along the lipstick, tracing the highway they were on again and again, as if to hurry their journey on. They were on the road. That was all that mattered. Kerouac take that! "We should call since we're going to be late."

"Pay phone's 'bout sixty miles back." Rebel thought of tundra and stomped her feet. A pack of wolves howling out on the tundra. But nothing was there. Nothing was anywhere.

"Here comes one." Chyna jumped up and started waving. She twirled in the slush of the road. Her red and purple tapestry coat sweeping through the air as she tried to conjure a ride. The man slowed down enough to look at them as if they were crazy. They were crazy.

Wolves had more sense.

Stranded on the fucking road.

It was how Rebel imagined tundra, a big white ocean. And the sky — one could get lost in that sky.

Chyna bit her fingernails and looked down the road willing a car, a truck, a tractor, anything with wheels and heat to come their way. "Send us an angel," she said. An angel with diesel wings to fly us through this sky, this big, big sky. She wanted to be there now! If only the land wrinkled like a map they could be there in a blink and a fold. She smiled sweetly at the next two cars — a half an hour apart — stuck her tongue out at the third.

Rebel's teal green and pink poncho flapped as if she was trying to take off instead of trying to keep warm. They were the only color in the land.

They ignored the next truck and the next one. Rebel took the rejection personally, and hated everything. Rebel was a stupid name anyway, even if it had stuck. She wanted to get rid of it just like she wanted to get rid of the smell of the road. She was bored. Bored.

Chyna wanted to shut her eyes to the sun and snow, and wished for a stone pillow. There was nothing to miss—you could see a car coming fifteen minutes before it arrived. She blinked and dozed half-standing.

They had barely spoken since the last ride.

"Chyna!" Rebel was talking at her. "Chyna, come on!" Rebel was running, knapsack in hand, toward yet another mud and salt-strewn pick-up truck stopped in the middle of the road. Why not stop in the middle? There was no place to pull over and nobody around.

Chyna reached for her backpack and guitar case: don't put your bag in the trunk, you might have to jump out; wait for your hitchhiking partner; never get in alone, get in together; make sure the locks aren't electric; if you don't like the person's look don't get in; you can say no thanks and catch the next ride; there's always another ride—except when there isn't.

Rebel was almost there. The door opened. She tossed her bags in. Wait, Chyna thought. Rebel started to climb inside. Wait, for me. The wind shoved her backwards then forwards then it pushed at the car door. Rebel backed out and held it steady. Oily slush spattered the inside of her jeans as she ran unevenly down the middle of the road. Breathless, Chyna climbed over the bags, crawling in between the seats.

They didn't look at his face, didn't want to dislike his looks —they wanted the ride. "I'm just going down the road apiece. There's a crossroads there." They thanked him, thawed. The heat blasted through them. He drove fast across the tundra where there were no houses. No cars. No where. Every once in awhile there was the beginning of a fence that went for a long time until it ended. "I raise cattle." Fifteen minutes, about twenty miles later by Chyna's calculation, he let them out at the crossroads. Twenty miles closer. Chyna checked her watch but it said nothing about time.

The sky was still big. The tundra endlessly endless. They watched his car pull up the road he called a crossroads; there was no one coming. No one for miles and after awhile even his car disappeared.

* * *

Chyna gave up her calculations and forgot about destiny. Rebel succumbed to despair, temporarily. We'll be here until spring thaw. They thought things but said nothing to each other about their thoughts.

The truck blended in against the dirty snow all around it. No one ran to catch it because it wasn't going anywhere fast, and if it had wings they were strapped on with chicken wire and shock cords. The cab was stuffy and barely fit three people and smelt of gas and oil. "I'm goin' to the end of this." He had gold eyes and gold skin and said his name. They said their names and settled in as best they could. The heater clattered stale air at them and they talked about wolves and snakes and the possibility of sex. He wanted some; they didn't.

Chyna sat above the gearshift on a hard piece of plastic and helped him shift into four-wheel drive to get through the drifting snow gathering as the wind picked up outside. Snow Devils whipped across the stage of the plains obscuring the road in their mad-dance. She leaned against the sleeping bag and Rebel's pack until her head lolled to one side and her eyes rolled up inside her head. She stared at the vastness on the inside of her eyelids as Rebel said something more about wolves; Curtis something more about snakes. Then they were talking about other things: hitching and prejudice, inflation and Cambodia, how it was happening again.

"Were you in Nam?" they asked.

The truck bounced amid potholes and roadside rubble.

Rebel drew two pictures, one of the gold-skinned black man with white hair and one of the sky and the tundra being plucked right out of it. Chyna dreamt until her head ached with diesel fumes and rattling doors, and when she woke up they had gone no farther than before, except the clocks had advanced and the sun seemed to have a different slant. "This here is prairie," he said and that explained everything.

They were ever driving across it, past fences and fence posts and occasionally a small town that disappeared along the vast edge of the horizon an hour after they left it. It was as long and wide as sky but a different color, sometimes white sometimes greenish-brown. Chyna was impatient for the road but it was the road they were on — she had no idea it could be so boring. They drove through the state forever.

On CB he hooked the girls up with truckers heading for Spokane. "They ain't hookers," he said, then dropped them off in the Northern part where it stopped being flat and the mountains began and it got even colder. Rebel gave him the picture she had drawn; she had written, Morning is Coming, underneath her version of the sky. He put the picture on his dashboard and after stretching a moment crawled back into the cab — he was going to Canada and they wondered if they should be going too.

Night shifted along the horizon, and stars were knocked out by mountains hemming in the sky—the same sky it had always been only now it looked different.

* * *

The No Hitchhiking sign had stories on it, some faded beyond the printed word, others freshly written: six hours at this damn exit; eight days and still no ride; 'Deadmen's Exit' if we don't get a ride and some food we'll be dead here when you read this; two days, we won't make it eight days; if the Deadmen got a ride we should too?; Spokane is God's joke on hitchers.

They opened their packs, wrapped up in layers of clothes and waited. Just after four in the morning the air died and the last scrap of heat was sucked off the earth. They cried quietly and separately — it was that cold.

* * *

"Where are we?" Chyna asked.
"Somewhere in the middle."

* * *

Like a spirit going fast-forward through the night, two lights hurried away from the horizon as the horizon began to shift from dark black to dark gray. It took forever to stop, and raced backwards with screeching brakes. The door opened and Latin music came gyrating out across the road offering a fiesta, a siesta inside.

The driver looked at Rebel's poncho, disappointed. "We thought you were Mexican."

They got in anyway. Inside, it was south-of-the-border warm. Outside the land was no longer prairie, no longer tundra, just land—not vast, not typical, not memorable—awash at a hundred miles an hour, like one of Rebel's watercolors.

The brothers sang Mexican songs while racing down the dawn. They sang the chill from their blood. Cradled by the sway of the Cadillac and softly foreign voices, warmth like tequila began to flow through their dreams and the sky finally turned peach. When they awoke there was a city in the distance. It was day, and the day before felt as if it had never existed. Day and night were miraged into twenty-eight hours on the road, fast becoming thirty-six.

Rebel drew a picture of the Cadillac on a pair of wings and

left it in the back seat for them to find later. Then they were out-side again and it was morning. They were in the north of the country and heading south in a few days. They were on the West Coast and had left the Midwest behind them. They had arrived, but it no longer felt like it was supposed to. Sleeping under a roof, bathing in a hot bath and gazing at a shallow sky felt false and detached from the journey outside — the chill of womb-light traffic. They paced the beach and the town like caged cats, big-cats looking out from self-imposed captivity.

It didn't call to them romantically. There was no siren's song. It just waited for them to quit resting, to get back on like after fal-ling off a horse. They had to do it.

They weren't *racing* home — they were going there at some point, but in a round-about-it way. For now, home was not a place where the hang glider, resting in the living room, gave journeys of dreams. Home was where the road took them.

It was alive. Get back on, it taunted them. Thirty-eight hours is nothing — you have months to go. It doesn't matter that you're do-ing it different from those before you — all that's important is, you go, man, go, because in a few years it won't be happening this way anymore.

That was the point, wasn't it? To be in it before it was over.

And after first touching down in Canada — just so they could say they went from one end to the other — they did it. The whole thing, in one breath:

Coasting on one-eyed pirates seacaptains russianimmigrants vietnamvets mexicansmugglers draftdodgers jetsetters Vedanta-temples and avocados, sleeping in redwoodtrees on graveyard-beaches underbridges and theHollywoodsign, they stole toiletpa-per cheesedisplays, fedstraycats starvingdogs and winos hard-boiled eggs and tortillas — hitching half way around this country in macktruckstoyotapickupscadillacs and subarus…

…one very long ride home.

notes on contributors

Anne C. Barnhill was awarded an Emerging Artist Grant from the Greensboro Arts Council and a Regional Artist Grant from the Arts Council of Winston-Salem and Forsyth County. Her poetry and fiction have appeared in several literary magazines and anthologies, including *Mt. Olive Review, Artemis, Crucible,* and the *O'Henry Festival Stories of 1995*. She has taught creative writing at Guildford Technical Community College and at the University of North Carolina at Greensboro, and is currently in the MFA program at UNC-Wilmington. Barnhill lives in Kernersville, North Carolina.

Joseph Bathanti won the 2000-2001 Carolina Novel Award. His novel, *East Liberty,* was published in the fall of 2001 by Banks Channel Press in Wilmington, NC. Bathanti served as a North Carolina Visiting Artist. He has published four books of poetry, and many works of fiction, nonfiction and literary criticism. He came to North Carolina in 1976 as a VISTA Volunteer to work with prison inmates, a population he continues to serve today. Bathanti is presently a North Carolina Arts Council Touring Artist and an Assistant Professor of Creative Writing at Appalachian State University. He lives Statesville, NC.

Kim Church received a North Carolina Arts Council literary fellowship in 1997 and residency fellowships from the Virginia Center for the Creative Arts in 1998 and 2000. Her fiction has appeared in a variety of publications, including *Mississippi Review, Northern Lights,* and the 1997 anthology *Voices from*

Home. She is an attorney, currently at work on her first novel. Church lives in Raleigh, NC.

Ed Devany won the Wachovia Playwright's Award in 1994 and a Durham Arts Council Emerging Artist grant that same year. After a long career in television where he received 13 Emmy nominations for his work, Devany came to North Carolina as a Visiting Artist for the North Carolina Arts Council, serving around the state for the next six years. He has been a finalist in screen writing competitions at Writers Guild of America, the Eugene O'Neill Foundation, Sundance and others. In the last ten years he has published in *Sandhills Review, The State, The Pilot,* and *The Independent.* Devany lives in Chapel Hill, North Carolina.

Ellen Devlin has won national and international awards for her feature articles, which have appeared in more than 200 newspapers. Her novel, *Hide and Seek*, published by G.P. Putnam's Sons in 1986, was re-released by Pocket Books in 1988. She holds an MFA in creative writing from the University of North Carolina, Greensboro and was a North Carolina Artist Grant Award Recipient. Presently she is employed as a senior science writer/editor at Family Health International in Research Triangle Park, NC. Devlin lives in Chapel Hill, NC.

Christopher Farran was awarded a North Carolina Regional Artist Hub Grant in 1997 from the Triad Arts Council. Two of his books were published in 2000: a novel, *Houdini and the Séance Murders,* released by Salvo Press; and a children's book, *Animals to the Rescue!* released by Avon. His short fiction has appeared in the *1995 O. Henry Festival Anthology* and the Madrid journal *First Word Bulletin*; his articles in several magazines, including *Parent* and *Road & Track.* He holds a bachelor's degree from The University of North Carolina at Chapel Hill. Farran was raised in Winston-Salem, NC and presently resides in Nashville, Tennessee.

Cassandra Gainer was awarded the 1999 Randall Jarrell Fellowship by the University of North Carolina Greensboro. She is a 2000 graduate of the UNCG Creative Writing program where she also was the fiction editor of the *Greensboro Review*. Currently she lives with her son in Baltimore, Maryland where she is a public relations writer for the Johns Hopkins Bayview Medical Center.

Kathryn Bright Gurkin has won numerous writing awards, including the St. Andrews Poetry Prize, the Ragan Poetry Prize, the *Crucible* Poetry Prize, a Brockman Book Award; and a Pulitzer Nomination for her book of poetry, *Stainless Steel Soprano* (St. Andrews Press). Her work has appeared in *St. Andrews Review; Crucible; Southern Poetry Review; Texas Quarterly; CrossRoads: A Journal of Southern Culture; ProCreation; Pembroke Magazine; Sandhills Review; The Dead Mule; The Independent; The News & Observer; The Lyricist* and in anthologies. Gurkin lives in Winterville, North Carolina.

Kathryn Etters Lovatt won the Robert Ruark Award for short fiction in 1992, and the North Carolina Writers' Network Doris Betts Fiction Prize in 1999. Her poems and short stories have appeared in a number of literary magazines, journals and anthologies, including *Crescent Review, Appalachian Voices, Elvis in Oz, I'm Becoming the Woman I Wanted* and *Grow Old Along with Me,* and she has served as the fiction editor of Carolina Wren Press. She has a Masters in creative writing from Hollins University and is presently a Ph.D. candidate at the University of Hong Kong, completing a doctoral dissertation on Eudora Welty and Flannery O'Connor. Lovatt lives in Hong Kong, South Carolina, and London.

Kitty Lynn is the winner of an Emerging Artist Award from the Durham Arts Council. Her fiction has appeared in Duke University's *Voices* and her motorcycle touring articles in *Roadrider* Magazine. She is presently at work on a book based on her experiences as a female firefighter for nine years, and on a collection of short fiction. Lynn lives in Durham, NC.

Heather Dune Macadam has been awarded a 1995 Winston-Salem Emerging Artist Grant and the 1995 T.E.D. Writer of the Year from the Henderson Times-News. For her play "Dear Dadann," Macadam was awarded the John Steinbeck/Alden Whitman Award for Playwriting, and named as a finalist in the Tennessee Williams One-Act Play Competition. She is also the recent recipient of a Carnegie Grant. Her first book, *Rena's Promise: A Story of Sisters in Auschwitz* was published by Beacon Press in October 1995; it is also in print in Britain, Turkey, Japan and Germany. Macadam presently lives in Sag Harbor, New York.

MariJo Moore was North Carolina's Distinguished Woman of the Year in the Arts in 1998, and in 2000 was chosen by *Native Peoples* magazine as one of the top five American Indian writers of the new century. She serves on the board of the North Carolina Humanities Council, and in 1997 was the project director for the North Carolina American Indian Literary Heritage Conference. She is the owner of rENEGADE pLANETS pUBLISHING, the only American Indian owned publishing company in North Carolina. Her published works include *Ice Man* and *The First Fire*, Heinemann/Rigby (England) as well as five books with rENEGADE pLANETS pUBLISHING. She served as editor of *Feeding The Ancient Fires: A Collection of Writings by North Carolina American Indians,* Crossroads Press, 1999. Her short work has appeared in *National Geographic, The New York Times Syndicated Press, Indigenous Woman, Asheville Citizen Times, Charlotte Observer, Native Women In The Arts, The North Carolina Literary Review* and others. She is a North Carolina Arts Council Touring Artist. Moore lives in Candler, North Carolina.

Val Nieman has received, among other honors, an NEA Fellowship in Poetry, the Elizabeth Simpson Smith Prize for

Fiction from the Charlotte Writers Club and various grants from the West Virginia Commission on the Arts. She has published a novel, *Survivors*, and her poetry and fiction have appeared in *The Kenyon Review, New Letters, Poetry* and many other journals. She graduated from West Virginia University and has worked for 21 years as a journalist. Nieman is currently an editor with the News & Record in Greensboro, where she resides.

Diana Renfro received a Regional Artist Project Grant from the Charlotte-Mecklenburg Arts and Science Council in 1997. She has completed her first novel, *Spanish Doors*, which is with an agent. She is at work on a collection of short stories and a second novel. Her published nonfiction includes articles about artists and travel. She is married to a kind and generous man who is helping her develop a family retreat and writer's colony on farmland in Ashe County. Two independent young women call her Mom. Renfro lives in Charlotte, NC.

Vivian Hague Satterwhite has won awards for her poetry from the Caldwell Literary Competition in 1994 and 1995, the Anson County Writer's Club in 1997, and the Union County Writer's Club in 1998. Her work has appeared in the *Lenoir News-Topic, The Lyricist* and *Branches*. Satterwhite lives in Lenoir, North Carolina.

Dave Shaw has received a Literal Latte Fiction Award, a Southern Prize for Fiction, a Blumenthal Writers and Readers Series Award, and a North Carolina Arts Council Artist Grant Award. His fiction has appeared in magazines and anthologies in England, Japan, New Zealand, and the US, including *The 1998 Best American Mystery Stories, Selected American Mystery Stories 2000, The Southern Anthology, Literal Latte, Southern Exposure, Carolina Quarterly, Stand Magazine,* and *New Hope International Writing*. He received his MFA in fiction writing from the University of North Carolina at Greensboro. Currently, he is the deputy editor of *Southern Cultures*, a quarterly published by UNC Press. Shaw lives in Chapel Hill, NC.

Robert Wallace has been a recipient of a Durham Arts Council Emerging Artist Grant, a Blumenthal Writers and Readers Award, and a North Carolina Arts Council Artist Grant Award. His fiction and nonfiction have appeared in journals and anthologies, including *Wellspring, Aethlon, Cities and Roads, The News & Observer, Spectator Magazine,* and *In My Life: Encounters With The Beatles,* among others. He is presently at work on his first novel which was excerpted in the Summer 2000 issue of *Lonzie's Fried Chicken.* Wallace lives in Durham, North Carolina with his wife and daughter, and is an avid Durham Bulls fan.

Luke Whisnant received a Blumenthal Reading Series Award from the North Carolina Writers Network in 1999. He is the author of *Watching TV with the Red Chinese,* a novel, published by Algonquin Press and re-released by Warner Books, Inc.; and *Street,* a chapbook of poems, published by MAF Press. His fiction has appeared in *Esquire, Grand Street, New Virginia Review,* and *The Crescent Review,* among others. Two of his short stories appeared in *New Stories from the South: The Year's Best* in both 1986 and 1987. He is presently an associate professor of English, teaching creative writing at East Carolina University. He is the Associate Editor of Tar River Poetry. Whisnant lives in Greenville, NC.

Printed in the United States
2378